Secret Desire
The Complete Collection

By Natalie Black

© 2014

All rights reserved. No part of this publication may be reproduced, distributed, or transmitted in any form or by any means, including photocopying, recording, or other electronic or mechanical methods, without the prior written permission of the publisher, except in the case of brief quotations embodied in critical reviews and certain other noncommercial uses permitted by copyright law.

This is a work of fiction. Names, characters, businesses, places, events and incidents are either the products of the author's imagination or used in a fictitious manner. Any resemblance to actual persons, living or dead, or actual events is purely coincidental.

This story is intended for mature adults only. It contains sexual scenarios, dirty language, hot action, and much more! Please store your digital files where they cannot be accessed by minors.

And above all – Enjoy!

Secret Desire: The Complete Collection

Vanessa has resolved to get over her broken heart this year and finally find a man who knows how to treat her. Just because she's a big girl does not mean that she's given up on love...although she wonders if she isn't just kidding herself.

When David, the trainer at the gym, starts to flirt with her, at first she can't bring herself to believe that he's anything more than a pretty face. Once they kiss, though, and she discovers that their lust is mutual, she could easily see him as something more.

However, David has a secret that Vanessa finds intriguing yet scary, but is her attraction enough to let her explore the wild side?

Vanessa hit the snooze again, but there it was, the persistent, nagging voice in her head that told her to get to the gym before she skipped it altogether, again. She groaned and sat up, it had been part of her New Year's resolutions to work out every day, so far that had wound up being three times but after weighing herself yesterday and finding that she hadn't lost one Christmas pound, there seemed to be no other choice.

This is the year that I finally lose the weight and find the right guy; it was supposed to be her mantra, her incentive to put down the ice cream and stay on the treadmill. She shuffled to the kitchen and made a cup of coffee and pulled the workout gear on, Vanessa was tired of waiting for both and this time, she'd keep her promise to herself.

Once she was on the treadmill, she felt better. She could picture herself on the arm of a nice guy for a change, not like Jacob had turned out to be. Just saying her ex's name to herself was dangerous. He was too sexy for his own good, let alone hers, and she had hung on for far too long. It was humiliating to remember all of the times that he had cheated and, worse, all of the times that she had forgiven him. The last straw had finally come when he told her that she didn't really have a choice - how many times would a fat girl like her have the opportunity to be with a man like him?

She shook her head no and tried to banish that memory. It had taken weeks to stop crying and even longer to stop wishing that he'd call again. Her best friend, Jessica, had even gotten tired of listening to her and that was a wake up call. Vanessa never told her that the diet and the exercising was a direct result of the terrifying idea that he just might be right.

Vanessa turned up the music in her headphones to banish all thoughts of the man who had broken her heart and used the time to check the gym for cute, potential dates, not that she'd ever expect any of the meaty, gym rats to take notice of her. She was just one more chubby, sweaty girl, but it was still fun to look. Some of the men here looked like they were torn out of a magazine, perfectly chiseled and every muscle flexed when they walked. There was one in particular that made her heart beat even harder every time she saw him walk by and today was no exception.

He was tall and blond and his blue eyes were not the first thing she had noticed but they caught her attention, after she had forced herself to stop drooling over the rest of him. He was tan and built like a Greek god and Vanessa couldn't help turning her head every time he walked by to watch his ass move in the skintight shorts and imagine him bare underneath. This morning though, he turned around after walking by and stopped right in front of her. Vanessa realized that he was speaking to her and she couldn't hear a word.

Flustered, she pointed at her headphones before turning the treadmill off and smiling nervously. *What would a beautiful man like him want to talk to me about?* She must have broken some gym rule, she thought.

"I'm sorry, I couldn't hear you," she said, as she stared into his eyes and tried to ignore the sound of her pulse in her ears and pay attention.

"You didn't have to stop," he grinned and she noticed that he had dimples, which seemed even more unfair, considering how delicious the rest of him was. "I just wanted to come over and introduce myself. I'm David, what's your name?" There it was. He had extended his hand and she finally had an excuse to touch him.

"Vanessa, nice to meet you," she slid her small, warm hand into his grip and noticed how powerful it was. The touch of his skin was making it impossible to stop the electric sensation that had started at the nape of her neck and was slowly crawling down her body.

"Nice to meet you, too. By the way, looking good!"

Vanessa felt her cheeks flush and hoped that he didn't notice. Hot men like David didn't come on to her - she must be imagining things.

"Just trying to get in shape," she shrugged, as if to say that it was almost hopeless.

"You have a great shape," he answered.

She watched as he stepped up to the treadmill next to her and punched a few buttons. She watched as he started running much faster than she could within just a few seconds.

"You definitely shouldn't lose too much weight." He sounded serious and Vanessa couldn't help but snort.

"Are you kidding?" she hit the button on her own machine again to resume walking, she wouldn't even try to keep up with him. "The only reason I'm doing this is to lose weight."

"That's too bad." David wasn't even panting, although his arms were glistening with sweat and Vanessa wanted more than anything to reach out and run her hand down his damp body. "I like women with curves, especially in back."

She had to hold on to the handles to keep from falling over. This gorgeous man was definitely turning to stare at her bottom. Vanessa was self-conscious about her ass no matter what she weighed. She could feel it bouncing behind her this very moment and she wondered if it were possible for him to be lusting after her the way she was over him.

"Really?" She couldn't help feeling incredulous. She and all of her girlfriends too were convinced that men like him sought out their thinner, toned counterparts.

"Oh God, yeah, bigger girls with curves," he couldn't disguise what he was thinking. He turned to her and stared. He looked like he was in heat and Vanessa could feel her sensitive places thumping in return.

"I like women that are feminine." He was moving his hands in an hourglass shape as if running them down her body, "It's irresistible, actually."

"Well, there goes my diet," she tried to crack a joke to break the sexual tension that was pulsing inside her.

He smiled and raised his eyebrows to her, "I hope so, Vanessa, but hey, don't stop coming to work out, okay?"

She thought that maybe for the first time ever, she would have a real incentive to keep coming to the gym and she shook her head,

"No, I'll be here."

Vanessa waved good-bye to him when she was finished with her routine and saw him wink. She was a sweaty mess, her long, black hair up in a messy bun on the top of her head, no make-up and wearing damp exercise gear that clung to her. How could it be possible that he actually wanted her?

She still hadn't answered the question when she got home, but she knew that before she went to work, she had to take care of the need that was spreading from deep inside to the rest of her body. Looking at him, studying every inch of his ripped body, from his rock hard shoulders down to his flexed calf muscles and everywhere in between had been enough. The flirtation that he had initiated had been too much for her to turn off without some relief.

She peeled down the skin-tight pants and the wet panties she wore underneath, lying back on her bed, she felt the twinge between her lips and at first, she remembered the last time that she had been in the bed with a man. Jacob had been a good lover in the beginning, just like the rest of their relationship, he had turned slowly into a selfish prick in more ways than one. Vanessa stopped herself, once she went down that path, there would be no turning back. Besides, she had just met someone who thought she was sexy the way she was.

She closed her eyes and remembered every detail of David, the flashing eyes and the dimpled smile. She pulled her jogging bra up over her breasts and massaged her nipples slowly, imagining that his strong hands were running over her skin and she felt her soft flesh harden once more. Her pink points were throbbing for his tongue along every ridge. She could see his blond hair, a wild mess as his head moved down as he made a wet trail of soft kisses to the crevice underneath her breasts and his hands traced her soft belly and reached out to grab her round hips.

Vanessa touched herself between her legs and sighed loudly. She was so ready. It had been far too long and she needed to get fucked. Her clitoris was erect and she was dripping wet, looking at his ass clench and release with every step had started the ache inside and now imagining him naked on top of her, about to suck on every needy inch of her slit would finish what he had started.

She remembered his hand around hers and knew that his fingers were strong and he would move back and forth with a steady rhythm over and around her fluttering nub, her breath came faster and faster as in her mind's eye, the tip of his tongue replacing the finger and she rubbed herself against him. His cheeks and lips and chin would be covered in her sticky juices, she could see him burying his face there between her lips, his fingers now kneading her hips and reaching around to her full cheeks to pull her closer.

"Yes, David," she heard herself say his name and it was too late to stop. The long, hard spasm rocked through her body and she felt the first wave of her release as she continued to sweep her clit in the soaking, wet circle that she was making around her swollen flesh. She would squirt, her orgasm would peak and valley and peak again as she fed him every juicy drop. She could almost hear him sucking her hard, his lips pulling her in as he assaulted her clit with his tongue. One last push of her hips and she was spent, lying in a puddle, holding her lips together to keep the sweet sensation from leaving her body, she moaned.

If only dreams really did come true. If only she had the courage to bring him home instead of just wave good-bye and run home to fantasize about him. As hard as she might try, she didn't think she could make that happen.

*****

"No way, come on," Jessica waved her hand to dismiss it, "he was just messing with you, Vanessa."

"I'm telling you, he wasn't," Vanessa hadn't been able to convey the longing in the flirtation with David or the next three that followed. She'd been to the gym every day since and every morning, she had been drawn to him like a magnet and he'd continued to torment her with his sexy smile and his perfect body. "You'll see, he's meeting us here for a drink," Vanessa noticed the twinge in her chest when she thought how unlikely it really was, but forced herself to stop that train of thought immediately. She'd never masturbated so much or eaten so little.

"So he's a trainer at the gym?" Jessica was a pessimist, although she would call herself a realist, "Do you know how many skinny girls are all over him every day?"

Thankfully, he was early and David waved at Vanessa over the crowd that was pushing through the bar ahead of him. She nudged Jessica with her elbow and nodded in his direction, watching her girlfriend's wide eyes as she stared in disbelief, whispering, "That's him?"

"Yes, I told you," Vanessa couldn't help but smirk, "he's smitten."

"Hey, beautiful," David grabbed her and pulled her close for a hug and she heard him inhale, "you smell so good." His face was in her long, black hair and his strong hands were running up and down her back. "And you look amazing," he said when he pulled away and stared.

Vanessa felt the now familiar tug of longing inside every time she felt his eyes on her and the gush of warm liquid that spilled in her panties from being so close to him.

"Who's your friend?" he asked, as his hand stayed on her back when he talked to her.

She almost forgot that Jessica was even there.

"Oh, sorry, David this is Jessica. Jessica, David," she made the introductions and watched them shake hands. Jessica was obviously as turned-on as she and when Vanessa saw her cock her head and give him a pouty smile, she knew that her friend was tempted.

"So David, Vanessa tells me that you like girls with curves, is that true?" Jessica was wearing a low-cut dress that showed her lacy bra that she was making sure that he noticed.

"I do," he answered her friend politely but turned to tuck Vanessa's hair behind her ear and run his hand down her back to cup her bottom, "and I especially like Vanessa's," and for the next hour, it went like that. Jessica throwing out invitations and David ignoring them, sitting on the bar stool next to Vanessa, he never took his hand off her skin, he stroked her upper thigh at some point and Vanessa could hardly breathe.

Jessica finally excused herself, she had gotten the hint and said she had an early meeting in the morning, tugging at Vanessa before she turned to leave, she whispered, "Okay, you win," and winked at him as she made her way to the door.

"That's your best friend?" he looked surprised and a little embarrassed.

"Yeah, I know, I'm sorry about that. I think she was just trying to figure out if you were actually a nice guy or not," Vanessa rolled her eyes, she would chastise Jessica when they were alone but for now, she was going to enjoy every minute of sitting with the most handsome man in the room.

"I am a nice guy," he leaned in close enough that his breath was on her face, "I'm a nice guy who is really horny right now," he murmured before kissing her lightly on the lips and pressing her dainty hand to his chest.

"Me too," Vanessa panted and wondered if she should let him take her home.

She still hadn't decided when they were only a block away, walking hand in hand, his fingers interlaced with hers, if she only listened to her body, there was really no question what the answer would be. She hadn't stopped wanting him since the moment she saw him. She just didn't know if her heart was ready.

At her door, she confessed, "I'd invite you up, but I don't

know," she trailed off as she shrugged.

"I totally understand," and his arms were around her shoulders and the kiss took her breath away. David's lips were hot and closed and soft on hers and when she felt him slowly open his mouth and clasp her upper lip between his before sliding his tongue inside, she sighed into him and gave him everything. Her hands in his blond hair, eyes closed, she remembered fantasizing about everything else but kissing him. Now it would permeate every waking moment.

"I really like you," he was holding her round face in his hands and Vanessa could feel her hips locked against his body and his cock had responded to their embrace. He was thick and hard and it was almost impossible not to reach out and stroke him through his pants. She bit her lip and wondered why she wouldn't let him kiss her as they walked up her three flights of stairs to her front door. She would have him unzipped before crossing the threshold and feel his naked, taut hard-on in the palm of her hand before she ever felt his weight over her on the bed that she had spent so much time in lately imagining him ravishing her in.

Vanessa stopped herself though and swallowed hard, "I like you too," there was more to say and much more to do, but she would wait. What was one more night of delving into her fantasy world?

She watched him turn and walk back down her sidewalk, his ass still drew her eye in the jeans and she whimpered and raced upstairs once he was out of sight.

*****

Vanessa gave David credit for the fact that she bounced out of bed every morning and couldn't wait to get to the gym and this morning was no different. They had made plans for a weekend date but she knew that she could never wait that long to see his dimpled smile. She needed her fix.

"Good morning, Vanessa," he was waiting for her near the front desk, which was now their usual routine and it seemed as if everyone at the health club had already accepted them as an actual couple. She got nods from other jocks and even a couple of the skinny girls smiled at her instead of just him.

"I have to tell you something," he said in a low voice meant for her ears alone as they walked to the weight room.

"What?" she was interested in everything about him, although his body was on the top of the list.

"I was having a dream about you when I woke up," his expression was pained as well as full of desire, "I was so hard," the mention of his cock made the images in her mind come to life, "and it hasn't gone away," he finished and he reached for her hand.

"Oh, David," she wondered if she should come clean, it seemed like the perfect opportunity to do so, "I want you so much. You make me crazy," for a moment, she thought she should ask him if he wouldn't like to take their morning workout to her bedroom instead.

Instead, she walked even faster than usual, even jogging for a few minutes, pushing herself physically seemed to keep the growing need in check although every nerve was alive. This beautiful man wanted her as badly as she wanted him, of that she was certain. Wasn't it time to put all of Jacob's nonsense aside and give in? Then there was the doubt that constantly seemed to shadow her, if she didn't fuck him soon, he would easily find another candidate.

The extra exertion had left her drenched, she was dripping wet with sweat and she could taste the salty droplets when she turned her head. Even her ponytail was wet and she sat, panting, on the bench, her eyes roaming his body and picturing them both naked.

"Are you going to take a shower here?" he asked and she immediately shook her head.

"I don't know," she hesitated, she had begun to feel more confident about her body over the last weeks but she was far from an exhibitionist, the thought of being naked in front of anyone who might walk in was still terrifying.

"You should, you really pushed yourself today," he stood up, as an actual athlete, his workout with her was only the beginning, "I'll see you in a little bit," David bent down to kiss her damp cheek before he turned to leave.

Vanessa went to the locker room and breathed a sigh of relief when she found it was empty. She stripped down quickly and tiptoed toward the shower. The large, tiled room was dimly lit and empty and she decided that she was brave enough to do it.

She finally relaxed once the hot water ran down her body, she could feel it cascading down her back and the brine washed away. She had taken the ponytail out and her hair almost reached the top of her cheeks and the shampoo made a line of bubbles down her body.

"I thought I might find you here," she heard from behind her. She opened her eyes and squealed, clamping her hand over her mouth before she alerted everyone. David was naked and the squeal was quickly turning into a purr as she watched him step closer. As much as she had stared she thought that she had memorized every inch of him and now she realized she had been missing the best parts.

His cock was the largest one she'd ever seen and he was achingly hard, his erection bouncing as he moved, slapping his pelvis, his hands were on her shoulders and his mouth was hot and soft on her neck. "We're going to get caught in here," she didn't know how she could think of anything but his perfect dick, but she was.

"I locked the door," he assured her and his fingers had reached up to fondle her nipples, just like she thought he would, he pulled both gently into two, hard points. "I can't wait anymore, Vanessa," his kisses were moving down her neck to her shoulder, "unless you don't want to," he paused; he really was a nice guy.

"Are you crazy?" she couldn't help but giggle, her hands were finally giving in, her fingertips brushed over the solid head of his cock and she could feel him drip on her as she touched him, "I've wanted you to fuck me ever since we first met."

"Vanessa, it's all I can think about," the words stopped, his mouth was busy, his tongue was out and had taken the place of his fingers on her swollen nipples, lapping up each point and his hands pressed her large breasts together so that he could suck them both.

Vanessa threw her head back and felt the water stream down her face, running down to him, her lips were swollen and wanting and the waiting had almost been too much. She could feel his enormous dick pressed up against her most sensitive places and she thrust her hips back and forth to spread her sweetness on his cock.

"Wait, Vanessa," he groaned and moved his hips back, "I don't want to cum yet," she watched him as David started to sink to his knees in the water, coming down on the tile, she understood what he wanted as he pushed her up against the cold tile and bent his head to kiss her mound. "I want to taste you so much," he gulped down the water before he kissed her hot center again.

Her arms were up, as if she were surrendering and Vanessa felt her thighs move apart on their own accord, her body was inviting him in regardless and when he kissed her again, it was further down her wet slit and all she could do was sigh. "David, yes, I'm so wet for you," she doubted that he could hear her whispering over the water, but it didn't matter, his tongue delved along her crevice and he swallowed all the sweet nectar that ran from her.

He licked from her tight opening up to her shuddering clit and once he fondled her there, her breath came faster and faster with each lap of his tongue. She was so swollen and hard, her bud had never been so full or ready and Vanessa knew that her climax would be quick and overwhelming. David flicked his tongue back and forth, slowly at first, his pace grew faster and his hands were clenched around her soft cheeks, pulling her closer to his face so that he could bury himself between her juicy folds.

"Oh God, you're going to make me cum," she was loud and she didn't care anymore, even if the door was open, there was no turning back. This gorgeous man was on his knees, worshiping every inch of her and she couldn't refuse him a thing. His tongue swirled around her clitoris faster now. The vibration of wet skin on wet skin was making her thighs shake. She felt the pressure building and the pleasure coursed through her like her blood.

He grazed her softly with his teeth and sucked on her now, Vanessa cried out, looking down at his wet hair, clinging to his neck as she watched him give her head. Drinking her in, harder, faster, the want had built to a fever pitch and her release came suddenly and made her melt in powerful, pulsing waves. She was cumming and every bit of her throbbed as he gulped down every last drop.

"David," she couldn't stop saying his name as she groaned and the last of her first orgasm left her, her knees were weak and she didn't know how much longer she could stand, she clutched at the faucet and felt his mouth move back up her body. He made a trail of kisses back up her belly, stopping at her breasts once more before pulling her close and letting her taste her juices on his lips as he kissed her.

"Vanessa, I could do that forever," he was pushing his needy dick against her wet pussy and she couldn't wait to accommodate him. She turned, her breasts were tingly from the cold porcelain now, her round, wide bottom was pushed up and her cheeks were parted. "I want to worship every inch of you," he panted, his fingers making a trail from her dripping vagina up to her ass.

She'd never been touched there before and she squeezed as a reflex, hoping that he wasn't going to try to push his girth inside her there, "it would be so hot if you would sit on my face and cum all over me again and again," she relaxed, he wanted to lick her backside as well and that she would be happy to give. He moved the head of his cock slowly back and forth across her opening as he continued to tell her his fantasy, "you could tie me up and make me your slave," he gulped and then plunged the head of his thick dick inside.

"Fuck me," she moaned and pushed her bottom up to take more.

"Yes, take my cock, Vanessa," he thrust in completely and she closed her eyes and felt the shower pour down her face and trickle onto her skin as he drove in and out of her from behind. "God, you're so hot, I just want to feel you on top of me, making me lick every inch of your beautiful body," he whimpered as he pumped and ground his way to her bottom.

She squeezed his engorged cock and heard the slap of his hips against her bottom as he rocked in and out, taking her deeper and deeper, filling her as she'd never been filled before, telling her everything he wanted to do with her. "Next time, you should tie up my cock so I can't cum until you want me to," every word was a groan and although she'd never heard of such a thing, she wanted it too.

"You're going to make me cum again, David," she wailed and she felt her body shake as her second, even more powerful orgasm rushed from deep inside to finger up and down, spreading from her core to her hips to rush down her legs with a loud "yes" as she convulsed on his meaty dick as he impaled her.

He hissed, his breath came harder and harder and she could feel his cock tense a moment before he exploded, knowing that he would bury his hot, salty load deep inside, "oh Vanessa," he said her name once more, his hands gripping her ass as he shuddered and finally unloaded his pent-up release in her juicy cunt.

They panted and groaned for another minute, staying in their position, she felt every wave as he continued to fill her with his climax and then, his cock started to soften and she moved to stand, feeling him withdraw before his hands moved up to her waist and his mouth returned to her neck. "You're unbelievable," he told her before nibbling her ear.

"Me?" she couldn't help but smile, the best lover she'd ever had thought it was all her, "you're amazing!" she was spent, completely exhausted and it was not the workout.

"I can't wait to be in your bed," he continued, "hopefully tied to your bed."

She shook her head and laughed, Vanessa had assumed it was his dirty talk, "so you were serious about that?" she asked.

"Oh yes," David turned her around so that they were face to face once more, "do you know anything about BDSM?"

"You mean whips and chains?" she didn't know anything about it, other than it seemed a little frightening.

"It's not just whips and chains, but yes, sometimes," his

dimples were visible once more and she thought she would agree to anything when he smiled. "I would love to be dominated by you," his voice trembled when he told her and she knew he was sincere, "I meant what I said about being your slave."

Vanessa shook her head, squeezing the water out of her hair and feeling the traces run down her legs, "I've never had a slave," she had to admit that she didn't think there was much that she'd say no to. He wasn't just gorgeous, but his cock was impressive and his tongue was too. She reminded herself, and he was really a nice guy. A nice guy that wanted to be tied up and abused though? "What would I do with you if you were my slave?" she wanted to know.

"Would you like to see what I would do?" he sounded eager and took her hand once she had turned the faucet and they left the shower room.

"I guess so," Vanessa was hesitant but she knew one thing. David was the closest thing to the man of her dreams that she had ever met and she was most definitely not letting him get away.

*****

The last two weeks had been amazing. Something had happened, something deep. Vanessa had felt it when he had taken her in the showers at the club. Something inside her had been awakened. It was as if a light bulb had been turned on. Her whole life, she'd tried so hard to be a good girl. It was as if being chubby had helped to make her shy and the most active part of her sex life had been her imagination. Now, with David, she seemed to be insatiable and she found that the more aggressive she was, the more he loved it.

Tonight was no exception and she had discovered a new secret, one more little tantalizing tidbit that seemed to push him even closer to the edge. She could even be a selfish lover. It seemed that David really got off on pleasuring her even more than himself. She had crawled up his chiseled body and sat with her knees pinning his powerful shoulders to the bed, her round thighs parted, wearing only a tiny pair of panties that were soaked through from their kissing. There was no place for him to go but to bury his face between her legs.

She looked down at him and the lust on his face was obvious as her fingers moved across her mound, along her wet slit. She asked in a low, husky voice, "You want to watch me touch myself, David?"

"Oh yes, show me, please," he was panting and he opened his mouth as if imagining that it was his tongue that was moving slowly along her sweet crevice.

Vanessa touched herself, moving her hips and her fingers in her own time. She tossed her head back and felt her long hair float along her skin. Her clitoris was erect and completely sensitive. Her finger made a slow circle around it and she felt the flutter inside. It seemed impossible that she could be this needy when she had been having so much sex. Maybe the more you got, the more you wanted it, she wondered for a moment - never having had this much, she didn't know. She was determined to enjoy every bit of it though, as long as it lasted.

David couldn't tear his eyes off of her flesh and she knew that the moans that came from her as she continued to touch herself made him crazy.

"Can I lick you, Vanessa?" he begged and she had already discovered the longer she made him wait, the hotter it was.

"I didn't hear you say please," she was only half teasing. She knew that he wanted to say it. She moved her fingers from her clit to her opening, feeling the trail of her juices pour out of her. She slid two fingers inside and groaned when she started to move them in and out.

"Please, baby, let me lick your sweet pussy." David would say anything she wanted and knowing that made her even hotter.

Vanessa withdrew her fingers from inside and plunged them into his mouth instead and watched him suck her essence from her skin, his muffled grunts as he licked her clean and looked up at her with a mounting hunger sent a shiver down her spine.

She moved her panties to the side and gave him what he wanted. Sitting on his face, she started to move her hips back and forth as he moved his wet tongue along her lips, parting them and finding her bud. She was so swollen and full of want. Vanessa had never had a lover who was so eager to please and so intent on giving her orgasms. When David sucked on her clit, she felt her legs shake and felt her bottom quiver with every movement of her hips.

She had stopped feeling so self-conscious about her body and she forgot anything but the sensations that pumped through her as she ground her hips against his face. He loved her flesh. He kissed her round belly and grabbed her bottom hard and pushed her into him when they made love. She had begun to believe that he really wanted her plump curves. Right this moment, she had stopped thinking of anything and could only hear herself crying for more.

"Yes, David, I'm going to cum in your mouth."

The first wave of her orgasm made her shudder and she gasped with each successive jolt as it ran down her legs. David's lips were wrapped tightly around her and she could hear him gulping down every droplet that flowed from her aching core and she kept moving, pressing her full, lower lips against him. The last bit of her release made her spasm on his mouth.

"Oh yes," she moaned as she moved and started to slide down his body. She needed to feel his thick, hard cock deep inside and looking at the glistening residue of her climax on his bottom lip and chin was turning her on even more, if that were possible. "David, I want to fuck you so bad," she purred as she made her way.

"Vanessa, turn around. Would you let me lick your ass too?"

She almost giggled but she could tell by his expression that he was completely serious and she stopped herself.

"Lick my ass?" she repeated it and thought for a moment. He had told her from the beginning that he loved watching her large bottom bounce and he had made no secret of wanting to hold and squeeze and knead her soft cheeks, but lick her there? No one had ever done that to her before and it sounded a little nasty and totally forbidden.

"Yes, please, it would make me so hot," David whimpered when he told her his fantasies and that had always made her give in up to this point, "you sitting on my face and making me worship your asshole."

Vanessa realized that it was going to work again and found herself turning on the mattress and then positioning herself, looking back over her shoulder, to push her bottom against him, pulling her cheeks apart with her hands. The tiny string of her ruined panties was the only thing between her ass and his mouth.

"You want that?" She felt so sexy with him that she even talked differently. She sounded as hot and bothered as she felt, pulling the bit of fabric back she teased him. She was just out of his reach and she felt him try to pull her down on his face.

He groaned when he couldn't and begged quickly, "Yeah, Vanessa, please, let me, baby."

She sat back and felt him ease his tongue up her crack. Her tender skin there, so unaccustomed to being touched, sizzled with the feel of him lapping in a slow line to her tight, little hole. David was burrowing his face between her cheeks. He was snug and completely surrounded by her skin as his tongue licked around her ass.

"Jesus..." It surprised her, the jolt of current that rushed up her body as he continued his tongue bath. "David, I love it," she cooed and felt her hips move to give him access as he slipped his tongue inside and tasted her there as well.

Vanessa had never felt the wet intrusion of a tongue there and it was slowly driving her crazy. She felt the puddle that she was making on his chest, the want was trickling from her and the feel of him sliding in and out of her made her pussy need him even more.

She stared at his erect cock as she moved back and forth, feeling his tongue enter her deeper and deeper with each push and watched him leaking fluid from his slit. His engorged dick slapped his pelvis and seemed to beckon her to come and take it. Vanessa reached down, arching her back as he tongued her inside, sweeping along her entry, tasting her. She grasped David's hard-on and squeezed, watching his precum dribble down the length of his shaft.

His moan was muffled by her skin but she heard him and pulled his cock a little harder. His head was engorged and full and seemed to grow darker the harder she gripped him. He plunged his tongue inside and was fucking her ass now with his mouth, Vanessa was panting and when she felt her body quiver she sat up quickly and took charge.

"I can't wait any more. Give me that perfect cock." It even sounded bossy to her and at first she wondered if he would find it too much.

He rolled up on the bed and his solid thighs were behind her soft ones and Vanessa felt him bend his head as he started kissing from her bottom up her back.

"Yes, anything you want, baby," he groaned and she backed up to give him her pussy when she felt the wet head of his dick pushing against her.

David thrust hard and it was her turn to beg now.

"Fuck me hard. Give it to me," she panted and she heard the slap of their bodies coming together and then apart as he drove his thick dick all the way home.

Vanessa gripped his girth tightly in her wet walls and she heard him call out, "Your pussy is so tight, you're so wet on my dick, baby."

"David, yes, harder." Her cries were beginning to sound like commands as her voice grew more harsh, her breath coming faster. "Yes, like that, I want you all the way inside me now!"

His pace was furious and Vanessa felt the sweat running down her forehead and she took every hard inch of him. David drilled her and she could feel him tensing. His heavy sack was taut and drawn up and she knew he would explode deep inside her when she came.

She squeezed him again and trembled as her release began. Her mouth was open and her screams grew louder and louder as her opening pulsed and pulled him in.

"Baby, I'm cumming," was all she could say. The waves were pounding inside and the current inched its way throughout her whole body. Vanessa wondered if she could ever get enough of his dick buried in her.

David said her name over and over and she felt him unload,

pushing a long spurt of his creamy semen inside. He was trembling behind her, his body sealed against hers, his hands clenching her hips and grabbing her to him as he let out a roar and finished his powerful orgasm between her soft thighs.

He was soaked with sweat and she felt his wet forehead rest on her back as they heaved, both of them gasping for breath. She slid forward to the bed and felt him follow. The weight of him on top of her, sticky with their combined orgasms, was its own pleasure.

"The whole bed is wet," Vanessa giggled. It wasn't ever just a wet spot - it was always so much more.

"That's because it's so hot," David said, kissing her neck and when she turned to face him, she could taste herself on his lips. She had given up on the idea that he was too good to be true and had decided that they were just absolutely good together.

*****

"So how is it going with the hot guy?" Jessica could not deny that she had a crush on David and was even a little jealous of the fact that Vanessa seemed to have really scored this time.

"It's great, actually." Vanessa couldn't keep the smile off her face. She was sure Jessica could sense her happiness even over the phone. "He's amazing in bed, too." She couldn't help but rub it in a little.

"That's not fair," her friend whined. "Okay, so how is he amazing?"

She knew that Jessica would want all the details and Vanessa wasn't sure how much she felt comfortable telling.

"Well, he's got that body, so imagine it naked," Vanessa was picturing it as she talked about him, "and his dick is even better."

"Come on…" She could hear the disbelief in Jessica's voice.

"No, seriously, it's amazing," she felt her cheeks flush as she thought of the rest, "But…he's into BDSM."

"So does he tie you up or something?" Her friend sounded more than a little interested.

"No, he doesn't want to tie me up," she remembered her own reaction to him when he told her what he wanted, "he likes being tied up though." The image of what they had done the other night came back vividly, "and spanked," she murmured.

"Spanked?" Jessica was trying to picture it too. "No, you have to tell me about that. You spank him?"

Vanessa couldn't deny that, as she recalled what they had done, her nipples had grown hard and she could feel them both rubbing against the satiny fabric of her bra. When he had first asked, she started to shake her head no, but when he got down on his knees and whispered, "I've been a very bad boy," she felt herself relenting.

"What were you doing?" Jessica asked.

Vanessa explained that she tried to channel her schoolteacher. She remembered watching the old woman take a boy over her knee and paddle his bottom as the whole class watched with wide eyes.

With David, it had started innocently enough, she remembered.

"I found a pair of your panties," he had said, looking up at her. It was an interesting mix of fear and desire on his face. He was breathing hard as he continued. "The panties you wore yesterday."

She realized that he was just pretending and decided to play along. Vanessa asked him in a stern voice, "And what did you do with those panties, David?"

"I was smelling them," he sounded like he was a young boy as he confessed, "smelling them where they were wet and it made me so hard."

"Oh that is bad," Vanessa raised her eyebrow and decided that there was no time like the present, "take your pants down now."

"Yes, ma'am," he said.

She watched as he fumbled with his belt, his fingers trembling as if he were really afraid of her in the moment. His pants slid down his muscular thighs and he pushed them across the floor behind him.

"Underwear too."

The thought of his hard cock rubbing against her leg as she slapped his cheeks had started to make her wet.

"Yes, ma'am," he repeated and quickly did as he was told. He was fully erect and dripping and she knew by the sight of his cock that he was loving this new game.

"Bend over my lap, bottom up in the air right now, young man," she watched as he lay in her lap, his perfect ass was bare and his muscles clenched in anticipation.

The first slap was light, just a tap really and he sighed. As Vanessa brought her hand down again, she noticed that there were some bruises on the underneath side of his cheeks. Was someone else indulging him as well? She couldn't believe how quickly her jealousy swelled and she began hitting him in earnest.

"This is what a bad boy deserves," she yelled at him and the sting as she hit him burned on her skin.

"I'm sorry," he was groaning and she watched as he humped her leg. Vanessa felt the trickle of his precum wet her thigh as he ground his hips into her soft skin and continued his admission of guilt, "I know it's bad that I jag off with your panties."

Even if it was just a story, the image of him using her silky underwear to masturbate was soaking the panties she wore and she knew that once the spanking was over, she would tell him to sit up and she'd fuck him right here on her couch.

"That's right, that's very bad, don't ever do it again," her voice sounded icy as the spanking continued. Now both of David's cheeks were completely red and Vanessa imagined that he'd have a new set of bruises on his bottom the next day. Her hand had started to ache and she knew that she would have to stop soon.

"I promise, I'll be good," he wailed. It sounded as if he were on the verge of tears and she stopped hitting him. Instead her hand softly traced along the hot, welted skin.

"David, I know you'll be good." The want in her voice was obvious and she told him, "Sit up now, on the couch."

She watched as he did as he was told. His cock was at full attention but there was one thing she had to know before she gave in to her desire.

"Tell me something,- why do you have bruises on your butt?" She wondered if she really wanted to hear the answer but it was too late; the question had already been asked.

He looked ashamed and David swallowed hard before answering, "I didn't know how to tell you."

Her pulse raced and she could feel herself glaring at him.

"Tell me what?"

"Well, I see a dominatrix," he said it quietly and she thought that he was shivering as he sat and watched her reaction.

"So you're fucking someone else, is that it?" It was stupid to be mad, she knew. They had never said that they were exclusive. Still, Vanessa had found herself hoping though.

"No, no, that's not what we do," he shook his head and quickly explained as he reached for her, "she's a dominatrix. She spanks me, beats me, actually."

Vanessa found herself imagining him bent over being whipped by a gorgeous woman. She was still jealous, but it didn't seem quite as bad.

"But there's no sex?" she had to make sure.

"No, Vanessa, I would tell you."

Her heart slowed down to normal and she smiled again as he spoke.

"I just want you that way. But would you go with me to see her?" he asked, sounding hopeful.

"Could I?" she had to admit that her interest was piqued.

"I'd love it if you did," David's hands were around her now and he was pulling her close, "now can I take you to bed?" he asked, about to kiss her.

"No, I'm fucking you right here," she whispered and flashed him a wicked grin.

"My ass kind of hurts, baby," he bit his lip as if he hesitated to continue in this position.

She laughed. "Good," was all she said before mounting him.

Recalling the evening had stirred her once again and although she left out most of the intimate details, she did tell Jessica, "I'm going with him tonight to see his dominatrix."

"Kinky!" Jessica added, "Shat are you going to wear?"

Vanessa smiled; they had known each other so long.

"I was going to ask you that!" and the two chuckled.

"Something sexy," was her friend's advice.

*****

David walked with her arm in arm up the sidewalk to the porch and they climbed the steps together, her heels clacking as they made their way to the front door. Vanessa was wearing black, high heels and she was just a little taller than him tonight. Along with her black, knit dress that clung to her curves in the right places, she felt that she was sexy enough to take on the woman that she still thought of as the competition.

David had noticed, looking over at her as they waited for her to come to the door, he whispered, "You are gorgeous."

The woman opened the creaky door before Vanessa had a chance to thank him and she was mesmerized at the sight of her. She was tall, even taller than Vanessa and she immediately looked down to see that she wore long, leather boots that stopped above her knee. She was a full-figured woman with blond hair that curled at her shoulders and dark, blue eyes that sparkled when she smiled.

"David," her full, pouty lips were painted blood red and Vanessa found herself staring at her, holding her breath until she heard the woman say, "Vanessa, I'm so glad to meet you."

"Thank you," she said and held out her hand. The woman's hand was strong, maybe stronger than David's and she found that to be very impressive indeed.

"I'm Mistress Ivana," she introduced herself, "please come in."

David and Vanessa followed her down a long hallway and Vanessa watched as she walked, her wide hips swayed with each step, the leather corset that was wrapped around her was tied up the back and the short, black skirt she wore beneath rustled with her movements. Vanessa found that her jealousy was gone but her curiosity was even greater.

She stopped outside a door at the end of the hallway and asked, "Are you ready, Vanessa?"

She nodded, not sure what she was supposed to be ready for.

Inside, candlelight glowed and threw shadows on the walls, giving the space an eerie light that wasn't necessary. Vanessa was covered in goosebumps as she looked around the room. Here to the right was a wooden cross with metal hooks at the top and bottom of each post, to the left was an exam table. There was a metal bench directly in front of her and there was a table covered in paddles, a whip, a pile of rope and many other things that Vanessa couldn't even name.

"Welcome to my dungeon, Vanessa. You may take a seat wherever you like and we'll begin," Vanessa found herself obeying the woman and wondered if it was simply out of politeness or if the woman could really make people do things? She was about to find out.

"Slave," Mistress Ivana's voice was much sharper now as she addressed David, "you know the rules. You are only to be naked in my presence," she snapped her fingers.

Vanessa watched him rip off his shirt, his eyes only on the Mistress. Vanessa had never seen him undress so quickly. His shoes came off, pants, underwear. Vanessa noticed that his dick was pulsing, completely hard and wagging for attention as he folded his belongings and placed them in a neat pile in the corner. Mistress Ivana noticed his beautiful cock as well and Vanessa reasoned that any woman would.

"Come, quickly, slave, get into position," her voice was sometimes soft as a kitten's purr and Vanessa watched him drop to his knees and press his forehead to the floor in front of her feet.

Vanessa was fascinated as she watched the strong, muscular god of a man that she had found so intimidating when they first met was shivering at her request.

"Very good, slave," she took a step closer, "now you may greet me," Mistress Ivana placed one boot close to his face and he kissed it.

"Up now. Get into position on the St. Andrew's cross."

Vanessa watched as the man of her dreams scampered to do her biding. His muscular thighs were parted, his arms reached up overhead and with a few, quick motions, the Mistress had his wrists and ankles bound to the wooden structure. His bare ass was well marked from the spanking that Vanessa had given him.

"Very pretty," the woman ran her fingertips along the row of bruises, "is this your handiwork, Vanessa?"

"Yes, it is," she nodded and felt proud that this woman noticed.

"This slave is very lucky to have you," the woman's heels clicked across the floor as she walked to the table to pick up a large, wooden paddle. "Let me show you what else you could spank him with and save your hand," Mistress Ivana smiled at her and Vanessa looked down her at swollen palm before clasping her hands together.

The paddle cut through the air and whistled on it's way back down to David's bottom. He howled in pain and Vanessa watched him jump as the wood struck him. "Yes, you'll feel that, especially on your bruises, slave," the Mistress sounded as if the thought filled her with glee and promptly hit him once more.

David whimpered after the last slap and the next made his legs shake violently. Vanessa realized that he might fall to his knees if he weren't so tightly bound and for some reason that pleased her. Again and again, the paddle came down with a thud on his prone skin and Mistress Ivana paused, saying, "Come here Vanessa, please, I'd like you to see something."

Vanessa stood next to the woman and could smell her scent and her leather and it seemed that the hot sexuality that she exuded carried a smell of its own.

"Now, see where I'm marking him?" She reached out and one long, red nail traced along the underneath curve of his cheek. "This is the sweet spot," she ran her finger up, "you don't want to hit his back," and then Vanessa watched as she stroked the back of his inner thighs, near his ballsack, "and of course, you want to watch the family jewels." Both women laughed at that thought and Mistress Ivana handed her the paddle, asking "Would you like to continue?"

She took the heavy handle and took the Mistress' place, raising her arm. The woman called out to David, "Now you're going to thank Vanessa for each paddle she gives you, is that understood, David?"

"Yes ma'am," he addressed her as he had Vanessa the night she spanked him on the couch.

The first blow landed and Vanessa heard him cry out, "Thank you, Vanessa." The next came quickly and in just a minute, Vanessa noticed that his cheeks were swollen and the bruises had expanded up his cheeks. "Thank you, Vanessa," he screamed with pleasure as the last strike echoed through the room. His voice shook like his entire body did.

"That is enough for now, Vanessa, thank you," the Mistress took the paddle back and directed a question to David. "Now, do you want to show Vanessa what you really like, slave?"

"I'm afraid to Mistress." It sounded like David might burst into tears and Vanessa could hardly wait to find out what it was.

"Oh, don't be a baby. Your girlfriend should know all about

your nasty little desires, shouldn't she?" The woman had walked to the table once more and Vanessa held her breath as she pulled a harness up to her hips. At the center of the harness was a cock, even thicker and longer than David's and it wagged in front of her as she walked slowly back to her position behind him. "Don't you want your girlfriend to know how much you love a big dick inside you, slave?"

"Yes, ma'am," he finally answered.

"Don't you want Vanessa to bend you over and fuck you the way you need, slave?" she asked him as she rubbed something from a bottle over the head of her cock. Vanessa found her eyes drawn to the erection. Watching the woman stroke it up and down like a man would was taking her breath away.

"Yes," he murmured. Vanessa had to strain to hear David confess. "Yes, ma'am, I would love it if Vanessa would fuck me with a cock," he bowed his head as if he couldn't bear to know what Vanessa thought of the idea.

"Then we'll just have to show her how much you like that, slave." The Mistress held the huge cock in her right hand and pushed forward. Vanessa watched as David took the bulbous head inside.

David moaned. It was a deep noise of pleasure and she watched him thrust his bottom up at Mistress Ivana, to give her even more.

"Oh, you feel so good, you're so tight," the woman said, half inside him and Vanessa watched her hips rock back and forth as she continued to give him more.

"Yes, ma'am, thank you," David sounded so grateful and Vanessa watched as the woman fucked him harder, his legs spread wide for her, bruised cheeks slapping against the black harness, she was pounding in and out of him now. All the way out and then quickly, all the way in, it sounded as if Mistress Ivana was taking her pleasure as a man would.

"My little fuck slave, you love being on my cock, don't you?" she purred and gripped his cheeks harder, her red nails digging into his aching skin as she skewered him even deeper.

"Yes, ma'am, I love your cock, I need it," he cried out and the slap of her leather on his bare skin grew louder as she increased her speed.

"Oh, yes, slave, that sweet ass is going to make me cum," Vanessa couldn't even see the rubber cock anymore; it was entirely inside David. "Do you want to take my cum inside you?" Vanessa knew that it was a rhetorical question; she would do whatever she wanted to him now.

"Yes, ma'am, please fill me with your cum."

Vanessa wondered if he was squeezing the big dick inside and fluttered on it. She could see his smaller cock jolting from her movements and expected to see him explode at any moment.

Mistress Ivana moaned and her last few thrusts shook him and Vanessa could see by her flushed face that the woman was having an orgasm from taking him like that. The power, the ability to bring him to his knees like that, to force her way inside him and make him admit that he loved it - watching it all was turning Vanessa on in a way that she had never felt and was almost ashamed to admit that she had.

Once Mistress Ivana was done with him, she withdrew the dick and slowly released his bonds as well. Vanessa watched as David crumpled to the floor, just a sweaty, pile of heaving flesh at her feet.

"Good slave," she whispered to him, but she was staring at Vanessa.

Mistress Ivana had other plans for Vanessa.

*****

Vanessa and Jessica were both a little drunk and their heads were almost touching when Jessica asked, "Okay, confession time. What was it like when you went to see his dominatrix? Scary? Sexy?"

Vanessa still hadn't processed all of it. She had been a little intimidated by the tall blonde initially, but then she'd been completely drawn into the scene. For the last week, there had been many flashbacks; she couldn't even admit to David yet how much it had turned her on to watch, let alone confess it all to Jessica.

"No, not scary. It was actually really interesting," she hoped she wasn't too tipsy to keep some of her secrets.

"So, what happened? Whips and chains and stuff? Did he fuck her?" Jessica was so nosy and, most of the time, she was just disappointed when the details didn't meet her standards.

"No whips or chains," Vanessa couldn't help but smile, "I did learn a lot about spanking though."

"Oh, do tell," Jessica leaned over and held on to her arm, "By the way, you've lost weight, haven't you?" Jessica was almost more aware of what Vanessa weighed than she was.

"Not really," she answered. It was only a few pounds. She had, however, firmed up considerably and that she credited to the amount of sex that she and David were having. "David doesn't want me to lose weight anyway."

Vanessa still found it incredulous that he loved her belly and her big ass the way he did, but she finally felt confident that it wasn't for show.

"Yeah, rub it in," Jessica rolled her eyes, "Okay, back to the spanking."

Vanessa gave her the synopsis of what she'd learned about paddling and told her about the room and where and how David had been bound. She wasn't ready to tell her about watching David take the cock, however. She was pretty sure that he wouldn't feel comfortable with her friend knowing that little detail and she didn't blame him. Vanessa surely didn't feel comfortable telling Jessica what it had done to her to watch him like that.

"So they really don't fuck?" Jessica had a one-track mind.

"No, it's not about sex," Vanessa pulled her shoulders up and said proudly, "He's only making love with me. The Mistress is for discipline and bondage, stuff like that."

"Oh, it's making love now, is it?" Jessica teased and then made a serious face. "You know that I'm just jealous, right? I mean, I'm happy for you, but jealous."

"I know, it's fine," Vanessa had never been the one to be envied. Her pathetic love life up to this point had been more tragedy than anything else. It felt good to be the one with the sexy man who adored her.

Speaking of which, it was getting late and she had promised David that she would be over once cocktail hour was over.

"I have to get out of here," Vanessa finally said. Her phone said it was almost ten and she knew that he was a perpetually early riser.

"Fine," her friend had had enough alcohol that she was more

emotional than usual, "Pretty soon, it will just be me having drinks alone."

She didn't have time for this and Vanessa bent down, kissed Jessica on the head and said, "You'll meet someone too."

Was she an awful friend now that she had a man, Vanessa wondered as she was in the back of the cab on her way to her boyfriend's apartment. Jessica had stood by and watched and consoled as Vanessa cried after many break-ups. Vanessa blamed her new lack of empathy on the fact that she was so sidetracked by David and the explosive sex they were having.

"Hey, baby," he answered his door wearing only a smile and all thoughts of anything but his stupendous, naked body instantly dissolved. Vanessa was ready to rip her clothes off before he shut the door, but waited. She had a plan for this evening.

"Don't hey baby me," she spoke with authority, channeling Mistress Ivana as best as she could. "Get in the bedroom right now."

She watched as he shivered. This was what he had been asking for since they met and, now, Vanessa was finally capable of taking charge. He turned without saying a word and marched into the bedroom and when she entered his room, he was waiting, hands behind his back and head bowed, for her next instructions.

"Get on the bed, slave. On your knees," she pointed at the mattress and noticed the ache between her legs when she saw that his perfect, thick dick was hard as a rock and precum dribbled from his slit before she even touched him.

"Yes, ma'am," he whispered and quickly did as he was told.

His perfect ass was in the air and she noticed that his forearms were trembling. He was a little frightened right now, unsure of what she had in store and that was maybe even more of a turn-on than just the sight of him.

Vanessa got on the bed behind him and cupped his cheeks in both of her hands, listening to him breathe harder and faster and then the low moan that came from David as she moved her hands up, stroking the back of his testicles and then the velvety, pink skin of his crack. "Oh that feels so good," he pushed his hips back and spread his legs wider.

"I know what you want, David," Vanessa was trying to keep herself from reaching around and taking his enormous erection in her hand; she had to wait. She was going to make him do that himself.

"Yes, please, ma'am," he was moving his ass back and forth for her as if she were already fucking him.

Vanessa had brought her large purse with her and reached inside. The bottle was on top and she opened it, squirted some lube on two fingers and began to circle his anus with the wet jelly. David shuddered and begged her, "Yes, take me, fill me up."

"Is that what you need, David? For me to fuck you?" she kept her voice low and husky and tried to ignore the thudding in her panties, her own need growing every second.

"God, yes, I want it so bad." His sides were moving quickly as he panted and when she plunged the two fingers inside him, he cried out in delight.

"I'm going to fuck you so good, David," Vanessa had bought a toy specifically for this purpose. The thought of taking him from behind had kept her wet and wanting ever since she saw Mistress Ivana penetrate him.

"Yes, I'm your cock slave," he agreed with a whimper, "Oh please, give me your cock."

Vanessa withdrew her fingers and pulled out the long, thick cock-shaped toy that the woman at the adult bookstore had assured her would 'rock his world'. It was bigger than his own cock and the head was not only wide but long. She had wondered ever since she had bought it, how much of the dick he could actually take. It had kept her simmering to imagine it.

She wet the tip of the toy and pressed it against his anus, asking, "Do you feel how big my cock is?" She had never felt so masculine or powerful and it was coursing through her body.

"Oh, it's huge," he rocked back and forth, obviously impatient to be filled. "Make me take it all," he begged in a breathy whisper.

Slowly, she inserted her toy and watched his asshole open up wider and wider to take the huge head inside. Hearing David gasp as he was stretched was intoxicating. He took the dick to the halfway point before his hand found his own dick and he started to masturbate.

"Yes, David, show me how much you love that, my cock slave," she improvised from Mistress Ivana's dialogue, "You want more?"

They both knew she was going to give him every inch of it but he answered with a wail, "Yes, bury it in me, please, Vanessa."

Vanessa continued to push the toy forward and was soaking wet when she saw that it was inserted to the base. He had every inch inside and was jerking himself faster now that she started to fuck him, out and then in, pulling up on toy to tease his g-spot and then plunging the dildo completely inside once more. David couldn't get enough and met her stroke for stroke.

"I'm going to cum, please let me cum," he could barely say the words. He was too far gone and Vanessa saw the stream of clear liquid run from the head of his cock. The wet sounds of his hand on himself had grown louder, almost as loud as the slap of the toy against his ass as she drove it back and forth deep inside him.

"Yes, David, you may cum," she would give him permission, unsure of how much more she could push him. Besides, she wanted him hard again shortly; she had a mounting need of her own.

Vanessa watched his ass as it squeezed, clenching his cheeks together. His pink opening seemed to swallow the toy hole and the roar that came from him was the sound of him coming completely undone. He splattered long, hot ropes of his creamy orgasm on the bed beneath him, saying her name with every push. David collapsed after the last wave and his whole body shook. The dick was still inside and she pulled out slowly before lying next to him. Running her hands up his back, she felt the sweat that coated him and she continued up to his cheek.

"That was amazing," she told him and felt his breath begin to slow as he turned to tuck her under his arm.

"I could fall in love with you so easy," David was staring into her eyes and Vanessa suddenly thought that she might have more power than she should.

*****

Vanessa had a voicemail from a number that she didn't recognize and when she heard the woman's voice, she felt a chill.

"Vanessa, it's Mistress Ivana, I've got a proposition for you and was wondering if you would give me a call at your convenience."

The gorgeous blond had a proposition for her? Vanessa shook her head in disbelief. If she only knew how much time Vanessa had spent recalling every detail of the hour she had spent in her dungeon…she was thrilled and curious at the same time.

Mistress Ivana answered on the second ring.

"How can I help you?"

"Hello, it's Vanessa," she even sounded nervous.

"Oh, hello. I'm so glad to hear from you. Do you have a few minutes to talk?" the woman wanted to know.

"Yes, please," Vanessa murmured, realizing that she almost sounded like David at that moment.

"I wanted to discuss an idea that I had the other night. It was clear that you were not only very interested in the scene but that you have a natural aptitude for BDSM. I have actually been looking for another Mistress that I could partner with for some time and I was wondering if that would be something you'd be interested in?"

Vanessa had clasped her hand over her mouth as she spoke, she was afraid she would squeal in her surprise.

"What do you mean, partner?" she asked. Suddenly images of herself in black leather sprang up in her imagination.

"I mean someone that could work with me. My client list has grown considerably as of late and sometimes I'd like to take a day off once in a while," she chuckled, "you know these subs can be so needy."

Vanessa didn't know but she laughed along with the Mistress as if she did.

"You could make a lot of money in a few hours here and there, you know," Mistress Ivana said.

"How much is a lot?" Vanessa was always on the verge of being broke and it seemed too good to be true that this could actually be a job.

The Mistress laughed, "You'd probably be amazed at how lucrative being a dominatrix is."

Vanessa wanted a number though.

"I make several thousand dollars a week, and I'd make more if I had you around."

Vanessa's eyes grew bigger and bigger at the thought.

"We could split things 50/50 on my clients until you have your own."

"Wow! That's…" she didn't want to let the woman know how excited she was, but she couldn't help it. "Do you really think I'd be a good Mistress?" she asked. She was comparing herself to the blonde in her mind and wondered if she could make the grade.

"Vanessa, you already have the look, so that's a big part of it.

All you need is the right attitude and a little bit of know-how," Mistress Ivana made it sound so simple. "Why don't you come by today after work and you can watch a couple of my appointments? I'll show you a few things, some easy bondage, like what I did with David. You can decide if it's something you could handle or not."

The memory of David bound to the Saint Andrew's cross still mesmerized her and she wondered if she should tell him about the woman's idea.

"Yes, I'd like that," she agreed and after she and Ivana hung up, she almost called David, but stopped herself.

What would he think about her doing the intimate things that she had done with him, now with total strangers?

She put her cellphone back in her purse and decided to wait. If the evening didn't go as planned, there was no need to tell him and she could keep a secret from him for one night.

*****

Mistress Ivana looked happy to see her and she waved as she held the door open for her.

"You're early! That's great, being on time is very important."

Vanessa nodded. She didn't want to tell the woman that she'd actually been waiting for thirty minutes in the car. She had been so nervous about coming that her stomach had churned back and forth the whole time and she almost talked herself out of coming at all. Most of her anxiety was about what she wore. It was the same black dress that she had on the first time that they met and it didn't seem appropriate anymore.

Vanessa pointed it out, "I didn't know what to wear," she shrugged and hoped that she hadn't blown it already.

Mistress Ivana cackled, "Oh my goodness, remember, Vanessa, you can be a Mistress in blue jeans or," she gestured at herself, "in leather from head to toe. I find that my customers are more responsive to me when I'm in the corset and boots," they both seemed to be wearing exactly what they had on at their first meeting, "but I am in charge no matter what I'm wearing and that's what really counts. Besides, I have something you can borrow."

Mistress Ivana led her to a bedroom and opened a drawer. She rummaged for a moment or two until she pulled something red out. "Here, this is perfect for now," she handed Vanessa a red see-through bustier, "I've got a waist cincher and a short skirt that will work."

Vanessa stood, waiting for her to leave so that she could change, but Ivana didn't move.

"Go ahead, I've got to get you some boots."

Vanessa felt her cheeks were warm as she started to pull the dress off over her head. She had specifically avoided undressing in public for as long as she could remember. She was so self-conscious about her size it seemed like a nightmare to think about using the dressing room at the health club or taking her clothes off in front of the doctor. In fact, it wasn't until David that she had ever felt comfortable enough to be completely naked when they had sex.

David - she grimaced when she thought of him. She had lied

about what she was doing tonight and he had been so sweet, as usual, saying "Okay, honey, have a good time. Call me when you're done."

"It might be late," she had answered. She didn't know if she could call him afterward and continue her lie.

"I don't mind you waking me up, baby," he responded, sweet as always. She had to force herself to stop reminiscing about it. After all the jerks she had dated, she hated knowing that now she had become the liar.

"Very sexy, Vanessa," Mistress Ivana brought her back to the present. The woman was standing in front of the closet with a long pair of leather boots in her hand as she stared at Vanessa, who was now wearing only her bra and panties.

She blushed, "Thank you." She had only just gotten used to David saying that to her recently.

"Let me help you," Ivana's heels clacked across the floor and she was behind Vanessa now, she had dropped the boots to the floor before unhooking her bra. Vanessa felt the material snap open and started pulling the straps off her shoulders without thinking about how close she was to being naked with this woman.

The Mistress was wrapping the red, see-through material around her waist and starting hooking up the back, starting from the bottom. When she got to her middle, she murmured, "Hold your breath, just for a minute. This is supposed to be tight."

Vanessa did as she was told. Ivana's hands continued up and when she got to the top, Vanessa felt her fingers reach around to her breasts.

"Got to get you in the cups," she told Vanessa, but her fingertips grazed Vanessa's nipples tenderly and she was immediately embarrassed at how hard they had both become from her soft touch.

"Perky," the woman's breath was on her neck and Vanessa felt the droplets of need run from inside and her panties were wet instantly.

Mistress Ivana helped her finish dressed and Vanessa was alternately ashamed and more and more excited as the woman's hands caressed her thighs when she zipped up the boots, lingering on her hips as she buttoned her skirt. She didn't understand what was happening to her body. She had never been attracted to a woman before. She'd never even kissed a girl in college when it seemed that all of her other friends had. Ivana was beautiful and she seemed to radiate lust. Vanessa tried to convince herself that it was the woman's job, but she couldn't deny the desire she had inside for more.

"You look great, and now we've got to get downstairs because Eddie will be here in a minute," Ivana said, looking at her watch. She was all business again and Vanessa tried to get a grip on the dirty thoughts that were keeping her from paying attention.

She followed Mistress Ivana to the door as she told her, "Now, Eddie likes to be spanked on the spanking bench. He's a college boy in his role play. I'm his teacher and he's been naughty," she smiled and Vanessa realized that Ivana must find some of the scenarios funny. "Once he's had enough of the spanking, he wants to have his prostate milked," she said as they were almost at the door.

Vanessa quickly asked, "What's that?"

Mistress Ivana giggled, "Oh, just watch. You're going to learn so much!"

Eddie was a short, thin man who looked at the two of them haughtily through his wire rim glasses until Mistress Ivana said, with one eyebrow high on her forehead, "I'm very disappointed in your behavior today, Eddie."

"I'm sorry, ma'am," he seemed to melt in front of the women and his shoulders slumped, "Please don't spank me," he groaned and Vanessa wondered if today his request would be different than planned.

"Oh no, that's exactly what you're getting, Eddie," Mistress Ivana raised her voice and pointed down the hall, "You're getting a spanking young man. Maybe that will help you to remember how to behave in my class."

Vanessa watched as Eddie made his way to the dungeon, dragging his feet as if it were the last place that he would ever want to go and Mistress Ivana smirked, covering her mouth as she spoke to Vanessa, "He always does this. Pretends he doesn't want it. If he really didn't want it, he'd say "red." Remember that," and then as she raised her voice to Eddie, "I want your pants and your underwear down to your ankles, young man."

They entered the dungeon and Eddie protested, "No please, not my underwear teacher."

"Why not your underwear, Eddie?" Mistress Ivana purred as she approached him, "does Eddie have a little hard-on in there for his teacher?"

"It's so embarrassing," he looked mortified and Vanessa hoped that Mistress Ivana wouldn't force him to show her.

"Pants down, underwear down," she smiled at him wickedly and added, "My assistant Vanessa is going to see that tiny boner of yours today too," Ivana said and Vanessa noticed the sparkle in his eyes when she said it. Suddenly, Vanessa realized that Mistress Ivana knew exactly what the man wanted and he really was just pretending.

His pants and underwear slid to his ankles and his voice trembled. "Please teacher, I'll be a good boy." His legs were shaking but he had already turned around to throw himself over the bench, his knees bent, his bottom up. Vanessa recalled David in this position vividly and once again she felt her clit throb for attention.

The spanking began and Vanessa watched as his bottom went from white to pink to red and finally a deep red with traces of purple, places where he would be hot and welted and definitely remember the pain. Mistress Ivana had continued to tell him again and again what a bad boy and listened to his promises as he whined about how good he'd be. Just as Vanessa wondered if she weren't pushing him too far, she watched his hand wander down to his penis and he began to stroke himself.

"Oh no, Eddie, that's not allowed. Do you have permission?" Mistress Ivana barked at him and he continued to cower until she told him to roll over on his back.

"What are you going to do to me?" his chest moved up and down quickly as he panted. It seemed that this was all new to him.

"I'm going to touch you, naughty boy, because I know you want it," Ivana had snapped on a pair of blue rubber gloves and Vanessa recognized the bottle of lubricant that she dipped her fingers into.

"No, you're not supposed to," he squirmed but his erection wagged at the Mistress and dribbled a perpetual line of precum, his mouth said no but his eyes were begging for more.

Vanessa watched Mistress Ivana plunge her fingers inside and she seemed to beckon him, buried in his asshole, pressing on his prostate. She continued the role-play as he kept insisting it was wrong and she continued to molest him. At some point, he began to touch himself and Vanessa watched as he quivered, Mistress Ivana had pushed him to the edge and it was entirely up to her if she would indulge his wishes. It was fascinating to watch as the woman made him beg for his release.

Once she had finally given her permission, Eddie came in long, gasping waves. His stomach and chest were covered in his salty mess and his mouth was completely open as he gasped. Every inch of his body was flexed and when he was finished coming, his penis had softened in his hand and he only panted. "Thank you, oh thank you Mistress," over and over he said it, until the two women left him to clean up.

Vanessa was impressed. She had seen a glimpse of Mistress

Ivana's control over David and she hadn't stopped wishing that she could exert just a portion of it since. Fucking David with the toy had only been a taste.

"I think you're hooked, aren't you?" Mistress Ivana was staring at her and when she looked back at the Mistress, her attraction was unmistakable. Her nipples were still hard from when the Mistress had touched her. No wonder these men threw themselves at her feet.

"Yes, I am," Vanessa understood what Eddie must have felt under her hands, "I want to know everything." She was including everything about Mistress Ivana in those words but that was far too shameful to say at this moment.

Eddie pulled out a stack of crisp money and handed it to the Mistress once he was dressed. He had transformed back into the serious businessman that he had once been, no longer a little boy, and he was clearly back in his own world. The change happened with each successive client that night. Vanessa watched as they would enter a man and become a slave. One was covered in wax and listening to him scream when the molten substance dripped along his skin was frightening at first, until she watched him ask for more. Another had his penis tied down into a seemingly impossible configuration and then Mistress Ivana proceeded to cover his body in clips that pinched his skin. The last client for the evening was tied to a chair and blindfolded. He seemed to hate every minute of it until Mistress Vanessa pushed the tip of her strap-on into his mouth, where he gratefully sucked her cock long and hard. His muffled sighs grew louder the faster she fucked his face. All of the fight had melted from him when she quickly loosened his ropes and bent him over the chair.

"Now I'm going to let Mistress Vanessa fuck you good and hard," she hissed in his ear, "you're going to show her how much you love to take cock, is that understood?"

"Yes, Mistress, I'll take all of it," it appeared that he had no choice, but by now, Vanessa knew that he longed for it and she didn't want to turn back now. Once she felt Mistress Ivana's hands around her hips, attaching the harness, she didn't want the woman to stop touching her either.

"Look at that," Ivana had one hand on her waist and the other on the rubber shaft that bounced in front of her, "You've got a beautiful cock," she whispered and then looked as if she would giggle but pressed her lips together. Mistress Ivana never broke character, "I can't wait to watch you fuck him."

Vanessa ran the solid head around the man's opening and asked, "Is that what you want?" in a low, commanding tone.

"Please take me, Mistress Vanessa," he whimpered and thrust his hips back to show her how badly he needed it. Vanessa felt the pleasure coursing through her body and she wondered if it was the anal sex or the blonde's hand that was still on her waist or if was being called "Mistress" for the first time.

Vanessa thrust inside the man and she remembered clearly every thrust of the toy in and out of David and how his body shook as he allowed her to violate him. This man was no different. He was panting and pushing back to give her every inch of him as he cried out, "Yes, fuck me," again and again.

"That's it," Mistress Ivana was pressed up behind her and the beautiful blonde's hands were starting to roam. Her breath on Vanessa's neck was a sharp, instant reminder of the thoughts that had been playing in the back of her mind all night since the Mistress had fondled her breasts. "You're a natural, Vanessa," she told Vanessa as she pumped the man full of cock.

Her fingers continued to roam Vanessa's body and when Vanessa felt her hand slide inside her soaked panties from behind. It took every bit of Vanessa's will power not to beg for more. It would seem very out of character as a Mistress, so Vanessa simply parted her thighs and bit her lip as she drove the strap-on inside the client deeper, and let the woman explore her wet, swollen lips.

"You're so sexy, Vanessa," Mistress Ivana was whispering and when her index finger stroked Vanessa's hard clit, she trembled down the length of her thighs. The woman's touch was light and her rhythm was perfect and Vanessa knew that she could easily reach an orgasm with the sexy blonde. Her first orgasm with a woman - it was something she had never even contemplated until this evening and now it wasn't just inevitable, it was necessary.

"I want to be with you, Vanessa," the woman had brought her to the boiling point. Her clitoris was so hard and fluttering, it was almost impossible to even concentrate on her words and the man who was impaled on her cock seemed far away. "I think you'll be a wonderful Mistress," Ivana spoke softly.
The circle her finger was making around Vanessa's bud was sending

a vibration through her entire body.

"A wonderful Mistress, but an even better lover," Ivana said, finally confessing her true intentions and at that moment Vanessa felt the hot sensation of her release grab at her and pull her in. If just her finger felt like this, Vanessa could only imagine her mouth. If she could make her cum like this wearing so many clothes and the strap-on, Vanessa knew that she had to be naked with the blond in the bed upstairs.

"Ivana, yes, I want you too," she only mouthed the words and as soon as Ivana knew what she had said, their mouths melded together, hot lips joined, tongues touching softly and then desperately. Vanessa knew that as soon as the client left, she would feel Ivana's tongue caress all the needy spots on her body.

She thought of David waiting at home for her. His face appeared in her mind's eye; just a flash and she quickly shook her head to rid herself of the vision.

Right now, he still didn't need to know.

*****

"I never see you anymore, girl," Jessica was complaining and Vanessa nodded her head, feeling guilty. She was right; it had been almost three weeks since they had cocktails.

"I know, I'm sorry," Vanessa sighed. She was sticking to her lie about being too busy with work which, she reasoned, was not a complete lie. "They just have me so busy at work now. It's like all I can do is work and sleep."

"Oh, come on. Don't tell me that you don't have time for David," Jessica sounded bitter.

Vanessa had to admit that it was the one downside to working for Mistress Ivana. She hadn't even seen David for three days now and her lie about work was wearing thin with him as well.

"Seriously, I haven't even been hanging out with David very much, either." Vanessa had been getting her needs met elsewhere, but just the thought of her gorgeous boyfriend's hands all over her still sent a chill down her spine. It had been too long.

"Well, call me when you can hang out then," her friend said. The women promised that they would get together soon and hung up. Afterward Vanessa wondered how much longer she could keep the double life going. It was one thing to lie to Jessica over the phone, quite another to do it face to face. She felt that her secret life was beginning to take over and she was losing control over the ability to keep them perfectly separated.

Her phone buzzed again and she saw it was David. She took a deep breath and answered.

"Hey honey. How are you?" She was still his girlfriend, as far as he was concerned, even if things seemed to have cooled between them.

"I'm horny," he laughed, "but I'm sure you know that already. I just really miss you lately. It's been awhile, you know? What is going on at work?"

Vanessa felt much more guilty about lying to David than she did to Jessica. He was so sweet and Ivana was supposed to be his Domme and she wondered what he would say if he could see the other things that she and Mistress Ivana did together.

"Oh, you know. It's just this big project," she mumbled. She was either going to have to confess or learn how to be a better liar. "And my boss is going nuts on me. He wants everything done yesterday, so I'm just scrambling every day to try and get as much done as possible."

"Well, tell me that you can come by tonight after work, please?" David hadn't been demanding at all, but it seemed like he was reaching the end of his patience with her too.

"I will, handsome. Tonight we will be together." Vanessa had no idea what that would be like. She already had an appointment at her real job. Now she'd have to take an extra change of clothes and wipe off all traces of the dungeon.

Her lies for the night were in place and Vanessa continued to get ready for her real plans. Mistress Ivana ran the business with an iron fist and she had never indicated, even with the change in their relationship, that she would tolerate anything less than perfection. Vanessa was always early and just the thought of being late sent her into a panic.

She knocked at the front door. She was under strict instructions to always wear street clothes to work. Nothing that would give away the real nature of what went on inside the otherwise-normal looking house. She had her own dominatrix wear that she would change into inside.

"Hello, beautiful. I really need to get you a key to this place." Mistress Ivana looked happy to see her and kept the door open for her and grabbed her bottom lustily as she passed.

"I would love a key. That way I don't have to worry about bothering you if you're in a session," Vanessa said, even though she'd like to have a key because it would also solidify what she thought this partnership was really becoming.

"Well, get dressed quickly, okay? You've got a new guy coming in twenty," Mistress Ivana was playing it strictly professional today and Vanessa couldn't help but feel a little disappointed. "Oh, and by the way," the blonde turned back and grabbed her by the shoulders - her lips were only an inch away when she whispered, "It's good to see you, baby," she said before they kissed.

Vanessa melted in the woman's arms. She had never been kissed like this and at times it seemed it would overwhelm her. Ivana's tongue teased hers and then she would suck ferociously on Vanessa's lips, one at a time, pulling at them with her teeth and just when Vanessa would cry out, her whole body fluttering with the feel and the taste and the smell of the Mistress, Ivana would be sweet and their lips would melt together. The women made ravenous noises as they tasted each other passionately, as if they were starving for the rest of something bigger.

"God, I love kissing you," Mistress Ivana murmured when she released her.

Vanessa was soaking wet and so anxious for more. She pushed her pelvis against the blonde's and felt the heat that was waiting there for her.

"Me too," she whispered. She knew that there was no time to drop to her knees and begin kissing the blonde elsewhere and she groaned. "I better go get ready," she said, resigned to the fact of it all. She could wait, even though she'd be counting the hours.

"That's my girl," Ivana said, and then continued down the hallway, back to her room. There were slaves to attend to, after all.

Vanessa changed in Mistress Ivana's bedroom and, in a matter of a few minutes, she was Mistress Vanessa. Her black hair was up in a bun. Her lips were a gleaming, dark red. She wore leather from head to toe and she inspired fear and longing in the various clients who would present themselves to her tonight.

The new customer was a nice enough looking man who appeared to be very nervous. He was pacing back and forth in front of the couch where he should have been sitting. Mistress Vanessa knew how to handle him.

"What are you doing up, slave? Weren't you told to sit?" She had a sharp, almost cruel tone to her voice when dealing with clients.

"I'm sorry, Mistress. I'm just a little anxious, I guess." He was actually trembling and Vanessa knew better than to giggle. Instead, she would give him something to tremble for.

"Get your clothes off, now. Fold them neatly on the couch and get into position," she snapped. She had read Mistress Ivana's note. The man had a shoe fetish and Vanessa expected that once he was curled up in a ball at her feet, her long, leather boots would help him to focus on what he craved.

He followed instructions quickly and was on his knees in front of her, still trembling. But as she sat down in front of him on the couch and crossed her legs, the sight of her in the boots made his small dick stand firmly at attention.

"See anything you like?" she asked him seductively while she placed her boot on his chest.

"Oh yes, Mistress. Your boots are beautiful..." he sounded as if he were in a trance and he began to clutch his cock at the base, staring and salivating at her small feet and curvy, leather-clad calves.

Vanessa moved her heel back and forth, grinding into his skin and bringing the tip up to push against his pink nipple. The man gasped and she watched as the wave of pleasure rode down his body.

"Get on the floor, on your back slave." Her voice was almost inaudible but he was listening intently for her next command and he obeyed without question.

She stepped on his chest and then his abdomen, leaving red marks on his skin. With each subsequent touch of her leather on him, the man groaned with pleasure.

"Do you want to lick my boots? Is that what you want?" she

held one foot over his face and teased him unmercifully.

"Please, yes Mistress," he gasped and opened his mouth, holding his pink tongue out for her inspection.

"Very good," she laughed. It would not be so easy for him. She moved her leg slowly down his body and paused to trace the outline of his penis with her toe. His breathing came faster and faster as she touched his sensitive, bare flesh with the boot.

She was very good at the slow simmer and Mistress Ivana told her this was why she was in such high demand with the clients. Vanessa kept the man on his back, on the brink of an orgasm for the better part of an hour, always promising to allow him his release and always making him wait once again. However, his hour was almost up, so she finally relented.

"Touch yourself now, slave, while you worship my leather." She was sitting now and the man threw himself at her feet and began to run his tongue along every crevice of her boot.

His hand jerked faster and faster as he continued tasting her and when he was on the verge of letting go, he begged her permission, crying out, "May I please cum, Mistress?" There was no turning back for him and she knew it.

"Yes, you may, slave," she said. And instantly he reached his climax. His long, hot dashes of cream releasing in waves, his cries grew louder with each burst from his throbbing dick and he splattered his orgasm down the length of her boot in his ecstasy.

Once he was a crumple of flesh on the floor, panting and heaving, she gave him one more command.

"Now, slave, clean up your mess. I don't want to see one drop of your cum on me," she snapped and he scampered to do as she asked. His tongue lapped up every last bit of his salty mess and Vanessa watched him swallow mouthful after mouthful.

"Very good," she rose and looked down at him with a mix of disdain and affection. "Get dressed now and I'll see you in two days."

She had reached a point in her confidence that she now told the men when they would come back. Sometimes she wondered where this inner Mistress had been all along.

When the man was about to leave, he pushed another wad of crisp bills into her hand, saying, "Thank you so much, Mistress."

Like the rest of the customers, he was anxious to leave and slightly ashamed once he was dressed again, but it didn't keep them from coming back over and over.

The rest of the evening went by quickly and when Vanessa's last client finally left, she heard Mistress Ivana ask, "Can you lock the door, lover?"

The best part of the night was just beginning.

*****

"Vanessa, come here."

Ivana was calling out to her from her bedroom and Vanessa hurried inside and closed the door behind her. She didn't know if she was afraid of being watched or just nervous about being with a woman, but Vanessa always wanted their lovemaking to be behind closed doors.

Mistress Ivana was already naked on the bed. Her long, blonde hair was fanned out on the pillow beneath her and her creamy, white skin seemed to glow in the low lamplight. Vanessa couldn't wait to run her hands along every inch of her porcelain skin. The kiss at the beginning of her shift had kept her in a perpetual state of need. Her panties were soaked through and she kept daydreaming about this moment all night. The blonde had become Vanessa's obsession and sometimes she worried about what was happening to her.

At this moment though, she had a need of her own to fulfill. Vanessa hovered over Ivana's body and kissed the woman once more. Their lips were pressed together and she could smell the scent of her wet sex rise as they both sighed into the others open mouth. Vanessa reached out to cup her hand around one of Ivana's perfect, large breasts and while the kiss continued, she quickly pulled on the puckered skin of her areola, making her nipple hard.

Vanessa kissed her neck, to the top of her shoulders, across her collar bones to her decolletage and then circled her hard nipple with her tongue.

"You know exactly what I like, Vanessa," the blonde sighed and gave herself over to Vanessa's increasingly capable hands. Vanessa continued tasting her full, perfect tits, holding them together now in both hands. She sucked one nipple and then the other, listening to the Mistress breath harder and harder with every touch of her mouth.

Vanessa needed more and she worked her way down Ivana's

soft belly, kissing her softly along each curve, working her way to her hips and then parting her thighs and kissing the top of her mound. Ivana was already so wet. She could see the spot where her desire had been dripping from her. The sheet below showed how badly she wanted Vanessa and Vanessa intended to give her more than she imagined.

Her tongue ran up the blonde's drenched crevice and she heard Ivana moan.

"Oh my God, yes," she would say yes again and again as Vanessa delved deeper into her heat, flicking her tongue around her pussy, inserting the tip, feeling Ivana's hips clench with each movement until she made her way to the woman's huge, erect clit. It was beautiful and dark pink, Vanessa had never seen another woman naked, at least not up close and she didn't have the experience to know if it was always this way between women, but at least for her, for now, she had a voracious appetite for Ivana and she couldn't wait to have her again.

When Vanessa would suck on her round bud, Ivana would always push her wide hips up and grab Vanessa's head, pushing her into her slit, as if Vanessa would ever stop or pull away. She didn't mind giving the woman control. It was actually kind of hot. She understood why the slaves would grovel at their feet. Vanessa would find nothing wrong with begging to lick the woman's delicious pussy if she had to.

Ivana never made her beg though. She couldn't get enough and, right now, Vanessa looked up at her flushed face while she sucked her clit harder and harder, her tongue moving up and down on her aching place faster and faster. Her lover could cum over and over, once was never enough and Vanessa had a taste for her this evening. Her first orgasm was close. Vanessa could feel her thighs trembling as she continued her tongue bath.

"Vanessa, fuck, oh my God!"

Ivana was pushing up, feeding it to her. Her clitoris seemed to burst in her mouth and the sweet spurt of her hot, buttery orgasm exploded in Vanessa and she drank and swallowed and kept her lips wrapped tight around the woman to pull every glistening drop from her. Vanessa loved feeling her thighs and her bottom clench as she rode each wave of her release and this was just the first climax, she planned on gulping down several more.

"Vanessa, let me get you out of this corset…" Ivana wanted to plunge her hands down into Vanessa's clothes and there was nothing that Vanessa wanted more. Well, maybe just one thing.

"I can't," she looked up from between the blonde's thighs and told her, "David wants me to come over tonight and I promised."

"Really? You don't want this more?" The woman hadn't said anything about her continued relationship with the hot man that Ivana only knew as a slave, but Vanessa felt that she didn't approve. "Come on, Vanessa. You can fuck him anytime." She wanted to monopolize Vanessa for the rest of the night.

Vanessa laughed, saying, "No, I really can't. Between my real job and working here, I have had no time for David either."

"You should quit your other job, and hey," Mistress Ivana took being a dominatrix very seriously, "What do you mean real job? This is a real job and you make a ton more money here than you do at the other place!"

Vanessa wanted to quit her other job, but she hadn't been able to talk herself into it quite yet. It seemed that her life had changed dramatically and at least her real job gave her some semblance of normalcy, as did seeing David. She glanced at the time and knew that she needed to leave in twenty minutes. There was just enough time to feel Ivana shudder underneath once more and kiss every sticky bit of her before she went to fuck her boyfriend.

Twenty minutes later, on her way out the front door, Mistress Ivana gave her one last kiss good-bye and warned her.

"You taste like pussy. You should probably do something about that before you see the slave."

The blonde waved at her from the other side of the door and part of Vanessa wanted nothing more than to run back to her arms and finish what they had started.

Vanessa checked herself once more before she walked up the sidewalk to ring David's bell. All of her leather gear was off, in the bag in the back seat. Her hair was down and combed. She had on her business casual khakis and the lipstick was wiped off. She remembered what Ivana had said and popped a mint - her alibi should hold at least for now.

"Wow, it's late, baby," he said when he opened the door for her. It looked as if he'd been asleep for a while; a line across his cheek and his hair was tousled.

"I'm sorry, I can go if you want," she murmured, her hands in his hair. Looking at him made her want to stay.

"No, no. Who knows when I'll get to see you again," he trailed off. He was trying to make it sound funny, but Vanessa could tell that he felt neglected.

His hands were around her ass as they quickly made their way to the bedroom. Their kisses were fast, almost desperate. David was hard as a rock and she felt him, thick and pounding, against her hip as their hands explored each other. Vanessa knew that she had never been attracted to a woman as she was with Ivana but she also didn't know if she'd ever wanted any other man like she wanted David.

She pulled down the front of his pants and purred as she stroked his solid shaft through his underwear.

"David, you're so hard," she whispered. She was driving him crazy just touching him. His mouth was open and he was thrusting himself back and forth, rubbing his dick in her hand.

"Get undressed for me," she asked. It was hard not to keep the commanding tone she used with clients and, even though she knew David wanted that, she couldn't bring herself to use it with him. That would make this work.

He did as he was told though and once his underwear was tossed aside and his shirt was off, he made quick work of her khakis and t-shirt. Laying her on the bed, he was on top of her as he began a long line of soft kisses down her throat.

"I've been dreaming about you, Vanessa," he told her as he pulled her bra off. Her large, heavy breasts came tumbling out of the satiny fabric. "I can't stand not seeing you."

"I know, I miss you too," she murmured as his mouth brought each nipple to a sizzling point.

"You should move in with me," he told her as his strong hand rolled down her round belly to her panties.

"Are you serious?" she asked, and wondered to herself how that would work with her other partnership?

"Yes, especially if you're going to be this busy, Vanessa. I want to see you every day," he said. His knowing fingers felt her hard clit through the wet panties she was wearing. "God, you're soaked. See, you should move in. You're too horny for your own good." he was joking but if he only knew how right he was, Vanessa was afraid it would be over between them.

"I am so horny," she said as she thrust her hips off the bed and wiggled the panties down over her hips. She was ashamed to admit that she was wet for the woman she had left behind, even if David was the only man she desired.

"I'm going to have to take care of that for you," he said. His first kiss on her wet slit was tender and his lips were closed but Vanessa knew that his tongue would find her and he'd easily bring her to the orgasm she so desperately needed in just a few minutes.

"Oh, David," she said his name softly as he began to caress her clit. She was so swollen and ready. The feel of him licking her in a slow circle was almost too much. The vibration was working its way through her hips and she couldn't stay still. She had to move back and forth and meet his mouth as she rubbed herself against his face.

Vanessa was shaking. Every nerve was alive and her clitoris pulsed with every touch and she tried to force herself to keep her eyes open and stay here, with him. She was ashamed to keep going back to her daydream about the blond woman who could make her cum even better and more than David ever had.

She couldn't help herself though and when she closed her eyes and saw Ivana's face between her legs, she quivered for a moment and felt her release build and build and she clamped her hand over her mouth to hold herself back. She would not say the woman's name when she was crying out in ecstasy. Her orgasm was hard and she soaked his face with her spasms of pleasure.

"Fuck me, please. I can't wait," she moaned. She wanted him inside her while her climax was still coursing through her and she felt David move up and rub the round, wide head of his cock against her opening, coating himself with her juices.

"Vanessa, you're so hot, baby," he said. He needed it just as badly as she did and Vanessa moved under him. In a minute, she'd grab his cock and push him inside. He must have known and the sound he made was almost a growl as he thrust deep inside her tight core.

Vanessa pushed and ground her hips against him. Their skin pressed together tightly, heating each other even more. She could feel David's heart beating hard against her chest and when she looked into her eyes, she could feel herself melting. It was way beyond just a good fuck and it wasn't just lust. She could see the tenderness that radiated from him for her and she knew that she would miss it terribly if anything were to happen to them.

She wrapped her hands around his ass and it was as if she could have enough of his flesh on her. Her cries grew louder and louder and when she felt him at the very bottom of her pussy she squeezed him tightly and felt her passion built to a peak. His dick tensed inside her and she could hardly wait to feel him let go inside her, the torrent of his cum pushed deep inside, the smell of him on her skin, the taste of his kisses - she wanted all of it and more. She wanted him to love her.

Vanessa said his name when she came and she felt the sweet, pulsing pleasure run from inside up and down through her whole body as she shook and clenched her pussy around his huge cock as well as her hands around his skin. She moaned again and felt David's release. She felt him push inside deeper still.

"Oh, baby, I can't hold it anymore. I'm cumming," he told her and she felt the steady gush of his climax as he filled her up.

She was so exhausted that she could have collapsed and fallen asleep right then, but she needed to get back to her apartment. Staying the night meant waking up even earlier. David looked at her with a sad expression as he watched her dress and make her way to the door.

"Are you sure that we're okay? Is there something you want to tell me?" he looked at her seriously and Vanessa almost caved.

There were so many things she wanted to say. But all of them seemed terrible at almost midnight and she had been lying since her first night alone with Mistress Ivana. Maybe they would make it long enough for her to be able to confess. Sometimes she just didn't know.

"No, David. We're fine, honey. Get some sleep," she said, smiling. She was going to tip-toe down the hall and go home where she could lay in her own bed and wonder what she should do next.

*****

The next night started with a session with both of the mistresses. The slave had requested that both women take turns abusing him and then fucking him with the strap-on. The tall, broad man was tied to the Saint Andrew's cross and after first being spanked by hand and then receiving a paddling, Vanessa saw that his bottom was bright red.

"That's going to leave a nice mark, slave," she murmured in his ear. Her breath on his neck was giving him chills as Mistress Ivana was preparing to flog him.

"You're not going to be able to sit down without remembering us using you for our pleasure," she gripped him by the back of the head, pulling his hair as she asked, "are you?"

"No, Mistress," he groaned and when she looked down and saw that his cock was throbbing and dripping, Vanessa knew that he was exactly where he wanted to be.

Mistress Ivana had the black flogger with the heavy, silver handle in her right hand and she let go with the first strike, the leather tassels slapping his cheeks with a thud.

"You are going to be so ready for my cock after you have been whipped," she told him in her sweet, sing-song voice that made slaves melt with their desire for her.

"Yes, Mistress," he howled as he took the strap again and again. When Mistress Ivana nodded at Vanessa, she took the flogger in hand and watched as the blond Mistress teased him, fondling his aching dick while he took the rest of the beating that he needed so badly.

"Should I let you cum when I'm fucking you, slave?" she pretended as if it were his choice and all of her subs clamored for the chance.

"Please, yes, Mistress Ivana," the man wailed, clenching his cheeks together as Vanessa hit him with the tips of the strap, almost smacking the back of his testicles.

"We'll see if you're good," she would keep it on edge and he would never know until the last moment if he'd even be given an opportunity to release.

"Please, Mistress, would you piss on me before you fuck me?" the slave was panting. Just stating his request made him almost burst from his excitement.

"Oh, you want to get your face all wet with my essence, nasty little slave?" Mistress Ivana gripped his face with her hand. "I think that Mistress Vanessa would love to give you a golden shower," she paused and turned her head, "wouldn't you, Mistress?"

Vanessa had never done this yet, but she had watched Ivana squat over several slaves and wet their faces with her liquid. Watching her had turned Vanessa on. Seeing the blonde bare herself made her want to run her hands down her slit and feel every inch, but she had never thought of doing it herself.

"Yes, of course," Vanessa answered. She would never show a slave that she was hesitating.

She helped Ivana take the slave down and laid him on his back, his hands now bound to a hook on the floor and his feet still shackled, he was helpless and couldn't leave if he wanted to. Vanessa loved seeing him squirm though, as if he hadn't just requested what was about to happen.

"Slave, are you ready to drink my piss?" Vanessa walked around him, letting him look up the tiny, black skirt she was wearing. In a moment, when she bent over him, he'd see the lacy wisp of panties that covered her wet lips and when she pulled the panties aside, he would see her pink and bare. It was the most naked she had ever been here in the dungeon.

"Yes, please, I want it so bad," he begged, shivering in his bonds, pulling at the ropes that kept him captive.

Vanessa stood over his face and let him stare as she pushed the skirt up to her hips and then bent at the knee and allowed him to watch as she touched the front of her panties, sighing as she touched herself. She looked over at Ivana, who watched it all and wondered if the blonde was as horny as she was right now.

Vanessa pulled her underwear to one side and commanded the slave.

"Now, open your mouth and don't waste one drop," she said before she began to urinate.

She closed her eyes and felt the little push as she started to let go. The sound of her piss hitting his tongue and running down his throat startled her. He was swallowing her quickly, unable to keep his mouth open the whole time. She heard her golden essence running down his face and Vanessa knew that when she was finished, he'd be covered in her scent and her wetness.

She was so focused on what she was doing that she never heard the door open or the footsteps as someone crossed the room to find them there, on the floor at the center of the dungeon.

"What the fuck! Vanessa, what the hell are you doing?" the voice asked and before she even looked up, she knew it was David.

He stood there, his hands clenched into fists. His eyes were on her and his mouth was twisted into something sad, heartbroken.

"What the hell? Why did you lie to me?" he shouted at her.

"Wait, baby…"

It was impossible for Vanessa to walk to him until she stopped what she was doing and now her cheeks were hot and red with shame. She couldn't understand how he was here. How had he known where to find her and how did he have such perfect timing to catch her doing something so intimate?

"David, stop," she pleaded, nearly bursting with tears.

But it was too late. He was walking quickly toward the door and Vanessa looked over at Ivana, who simply threw up her hands.

Rising from her bent position, Vanessa decided to chase after the man she loved.

*****

Vanessa had never felt so ashamed in her life as she did when she went running after him, having lost all of her Mistress persona at that moment when David's voice had turned her whole world upside down.

"David, please. Stop. Let me explain," she called out to him.

He had reached the door. She stopped cold. She couldn't chase him down the street, especially not dressed like this.

He finally stopped and turned around to face her. David's face was red and she could see the large vein in his forehead pulsing with intensity. Vanessa gulped and felt her hands shaking. She had never seen a hint of his temper before and it was a little frightening.

"I just can't believe you fucking lied to me," he finally said. He was talking much more quietly than normal but it was obvious by his tone that he was still infuriated.

"David, I wanted to tell you. I really did," she said as she shook her head to herself. Men had used this line on her in the past and she hated herself for turning into a liar and a cheat. "I was just afraid of what you'd say."

"So it was better to just hurt me? Is that it Vanessa?" His biceps were flexed when he threw his hands up. "You don't think I would have understood? Now I don't think I could believe a word you ever say."

To her, it seemed as though her handsome lover was giving up on her completely and Vanessa felt the tears in her eyes.

"Please, David, just wait," she begged. She would change back into her street clothes and tell him everything - the long hours at work that had been spent here with slaves and then, of course, there was Mistress Ivana. David was fascinated by the woman. Surely he'd understand that she couldn't really help herself around the sexy blonde.

"No, Vanessa. I'm out of here." He pushed the door open and added, "Have fun with whatever you have going on here," his voice was sarcastic and bitter and meant to hurt her.

She was crying as she watched him walk until he was out of view and Vanessa stood there, hands on her face, head bowed as she told herself that she deserved his anger. It was the worst thing that she'd ever done to a man and David had always been so sweet. In fact, he had always been dangerously close to perfect. Had she just lost her true love?

Vanessa wiped her cheeks when she heard the dungeon door creak open and then closed and she turned her head to see Mistress Ivana coming toward her.

"You okay?" the dominatrix asked her with a look of concern.

"No, not really. I don't know…" Vanessa sniffed and then remembered that she had left the slave in the middle of the session. She had managed to lose her boyfriend as well as a client in the last few minutes. She worried that she might lose her job as well.

"Don't worry. He's fine. He loved it," the Mistress nodded toward the room where the man was more than likely cleaning up and getting dressed. "How did David know to find you here?"

It was a question that Vanessa couldn't answer and she simply shrugged.

"I have no idea. I had told him that I was working a lot lately."

She could picture him showing up at her office and asking for her, anxious to get in a quick hug and long kiss, something to entice her to come by his apartment later. She, of course, would not have been there if he checked. And, even worse, her co-workers probably told him that she never worked late. Vanessa could only imagine what he'd thought as he discovered all of this.

"Well, that's not even a lie," Mistress Ivana's eyes sparkled and she gave Vanessa a wicked smile. "You *have* been working a lot. What would he be so upset about? Does he know anything about us?"

Vanessa hadn't even gotten that far in her thought processing yet.

"No, and now I'm sure he'll hate me even more for that, once he finds out."

Vanessa couldn't see David even giving her a chance to disappoint him further, not after watching her exposing herself over a stranger. It would just be added to the count of her misdeeds.

"I tell you what," Mistress Ivana put her hand on Vanessa's bare shoulder and, even in her distraught state, the warmth of the woman's skin on hers worked its way through her body, "go in the bedroom. Lie down and relax for a little bit. I'll handle the next appointment. You need a break."

"Thank you," she mumbled, hoping that on top of everything else, she hadn't just lost the best job she'd ever had.

Vanessa went in the woman's bedroom and, with one look at

the bed, and all the memories of what the two of them had done over the last days and nights in that bed instantly flooded over her. She walked over to the mirror and saw that her eye make-up had streaked down her cheeks and she tried to clean it off. It was hopeless. She was a mess and she curled up in a ball, with her head on Ivana's pillow. It carried her scent and Vanessa found it comforting, as if her lover were here, holding her close.

She must have dozed off and Vanessa woke up later to the soft hand of the blonde woman stroking her cheek as she heard Ivana calling her name.

"You're so beautiful like that," Ivana told her and when Vanessa opened her eyes, she smiled and momentarily forgot that she had just lost the most lovable man she had ever known.

"Let me help you out of this corset. You'll be much more comfortable."

Ivana's hands were picking her up, loosening the laces that bound her in the leather and she made quick work of the tight garment. The Mistress had her completely naked in moments and Vanessa never resisted. It didn't seem to matter that the men that came and went saw her as Mistress as well, with this woman all she wanted was to surrender.

The woman's long, blonde hair was touching her shoulder as her face came closer to Vanessa's face.

"I couldn't wait to get you alone," she murmured before she pressed her hot lips to Vanessa's. Kissing another woman had been one of the most erotic things she'd ever done, although it seemed like everything that she did with the Mistress gave her more and more pleasure.

Their tongues joined and slid together and apart, smoothly and slowly. Vanessa heard herself moan as Ivana's hands made their way across her shoulders to her full breasts. Ivana seemed to know exactly how to bring her nipples to two aching points with the lightest of touches and Vanessa felt how wet she had become just thinking about it.

The blonde released her mouth and started her trail of kisses down her soft throat as she made her way to her cleavage. Vanessa watched as the lips caressed her skin and then saw the tip of her tongue collide with her pink, puckered point and she felt her clitoris swell from the softest touch.

"That feels so good," she moaned and she wrapped her fingers in Ivana's hair as the blonde licked her softly and then closed her lips around the tender flesh and sucked her into her mouth. Vanessa knew that she'd be a puddle of want in minutes when the touch of the other woman would wander down her waist, to her full hips and stop between her thighs.

"I love to make you cum with my fingers," Ivana told her before her teeth gently grazed her wet point and Vanessa sighed, spreading her legs wider to give the woman access to her damp slit.

Mistress Ivana's expert touch was the thing that slaves craved the most and Vanessa understood why as Ivana slipped two fingers between her swollen, bare lips and she made her way slowly from her dripping opening to her thudding clit and then back down.

"God, yes. I love the way you touch me," Vanessa's said as her hips writhed under the blonde. When Mistress Ivana inserted two fingers inside her and worked back and forth slowly, Vanessa started to convulse and she could hear how wet she had become as the woman continued to fuck her.

"I can't get enough of you, Vanessa." Ivana's eyes were full of lust as she pulled out and started her feather-light circular stroke on Vanessa's erect bud. She knew that the blonde could easily give her an orgasm just like that. She was like putty in the Mistress' hands.

Vanessa laid back on the pillow and groaned as Mistress Ivana moved down her body and positioned herself between Vanessa's round thighs. The blond kissed her crevice with hot, closed-mouth kisses until Vanessa was almost on the verge of her release. It wasn't until Vanessa quivered with her delight that Ivana would give her the tongue that she found herself perpetually wanting.

Ivana's tongue circled her clit and Vanessa's thighs shook from her need as the woman took complete control of her climax. The Mistress slipped her two fingers back inside Vanessa's heated opening and flicked them back and forth as if beckoning to her, as if calling her out to let the pleasure pour from her body. The lips drank her in and the woman's tongue tormented her, bringing her to the edge, letting her wait, letting her feel the first pulse of her orgasm and then forcing her back down until she couldn't stand another minute.

"Ivana, yes, let me cum, oh, God," Vanessa moaned in delight.

In this bedroom, Vanessa was the sub and Mistress Ivana

always the domme. Even when they switched places, Vanessa was gladly her slave, carefully following the blonde's every desire. That's exactly how they both liked it.

Ivana lapped at her faster, her fingers increased their tempo and soon Vanessa was nothing but a sensation, a vibration that ripped through her insides to course through every inch of her flesh. No other lover had been able to bring her to the heights that she felt with the Mistress and it seemed that, more and more, she was completely helpless under the woman's spell.

"Yes, Ivana, yes…" She shuddered and felt the spurt that exploded from between her legs. Vanessa would give her wave after wave of her wetness and Ivana would greedily suck every last drop from her. She could hear Ivana swallowing down the hot juices that squirted from her and she knew that when the woman kissed her way back up to her mouth, she would share the glistening drops of her sweetness that Vanessa had marked her with.

It would be another long night, filled with passion, and it wasn't until the women were completely spent, naked and panting, clinging to each other in the damp sheets that Vanessa remembered that she had just hours earlier been caught betraying the man that had won her heart. The weight of the realization came crashing down on her and she realized she was too deep into it all to get off cleanly. Not this time. She wondered what would happen when she finally left Ivana's house and the dream-like trance she found herself enveloped in.

She had no idea what awaited her, and she was terrified to find out.

*****

"Hello, David…" Vanessa was leaving her third voicemail in less than 24 hours on his phone. She knew that she was approaching obsessive but she hoped that the man she thought she loved would at least give her a chance to explain. "If you can, please call me back. I know you're mad and I don't blame you…" She recalled being so jealous and intimidated of the ferocious blonde when they first met. If the tables were turned, she didn't know if she could forgive either. "But just call me back and give me a chance. Please."

It was still dark out, practically the middle of the night, but Vanessa couldn't sleep. No matter how she felt about Ivana, deep down she knew that it was all just for fun. The woman did things to her body that continued to shock and amaze her. Actually, just remembering the blonde for a minute made her heart race. But David was something different. What she had with David was something real.

Vanessa bit her lip and chided herself. She should have kept that in mind before she decided to sneak around behind his back and not only become a Mistress herself but to take a lover too. If she had to do it over again, would she have been able to resist the blonde's charms?

She knew where David would be though. If not now, then shortly. Vanessa found her workout gear in the bottom of the drawer; she hadn't been back to the gym in a while. She had never liked working out and her only incentive had been spending time with David. Once the job at the dungeon had taken up all of her free time, she had spent the extra hour curled up in her bed when she should have been working out. This morning, though, she would find him and give it one last try. It was her only choice.

He was already on the treadmill when she got there, and the sweat trickled down his face. His arms and legs were damp and Vanessa knew that he must have been running for quite a while to be this sweaty. She stared at him, unseen, for a few minutes. Every flex of his arms as he worked them back and forth, every line of his muscles as he moved - she couldn't help but think of him naked and on top of her. She regretted her carelessness at that moment more than ever.

David looked up at her briefly and the expression on his face changed to anger again. His finger poked at the button on the screen and he started to run faster. Vanessa stepped on the treadmill next to him and started to speak.

"I figured that you'd be here."

He shook his head no as if to tell her that she should go away and she felt her heart break a little more as he glared back at her.

"David, I know I lied, but there's a reason why." Vanessa told herself not to cry and cleared her throat when the lump in it became too big to continue. "Look, I didn't know what was going to happen when I first went to the dungeon and before I knew it, I was in over my head."

David hung on to the treadmill as he pushed the button again to slow down. He was breathing hard as he said, "Can you imagine how stupid I felt when I went to your office to say hi to you and the people there said you had actually left early?"

That was how she had been caught and Vanessa went through the short list of names mentally as she wondered who would have told on her. Probably another woman. Probably out of jealousy and Vanessa felt like kicking herself again for being stupid on top of lying.

"I'm sure it was awful, but I didn't know what else to tell you. Would you have been this angry if I had told you what I was really doing?" Was it just that she had lied or was David also jealous of the attention she was giving other men?

"You know what? Yes, I would have been upset but I really thought you and I had something special," he spat the words at her, "now I don't know if I want to even talk to you."

Vanessa stood with her arms crossed, deep in thought. She remembered Mistress Ivana and one slave in particular. He had come in defiant and cocky. Vanessa had been a little scared as the man puffed his chest and made his demands. She recalled what had happened next and felt a glimmer of hope.

"You know what? That's fine," she said as she stepped off the treadmill.

David was, no matter how gorgeous or how sweet, a sub after all.

"You don't want to give me the courtesy of listening, even after it was you who introduced me to all of this? Fine. I've got better things to do than chase you."

It was a dangerous game she was playing. There was a chance he would let her go.

Vanessa walked down the hallway, headed for the lockers without another word and it was killing her not to look back and see what he had decided. She heard his long strides behind her before she felt his hand on her arm.

"Hey, Vanessa. You're right. I'm sorry."

Vanessa clenched her lips together before she smiled involuntarily. Mistress Ivana knew men so well.

"You should be sorry." Vanessa turned to look at him, one eyebrow up. Her mouth was a straight line and she knew that it was the same face she used with slaves. "I haven't even been given a chance to explain and your behavior is inexcusable." She would go on the offensive and hopefully it would work.

"Does it matter that I love you?" He grabbed her hand and pulled her close, right there in front of everyone at the health club. "I was only angry because I was jealous. I would love for you to do to me what I saw you doing with that other man."

Vanessa was delighted and gave him a pouty smile. She supposed that it was time to confess everything now that she had turned the tables so well.

"Of course you were jealous," she was going to tease him now until he was malleable once more, "who wouldn't want to taste me like that?"

"Oh God," he groaned, pushing his pelvis into her. He was

rock hard and he had completely given up his position now. "It made me so hot to watch and then when I went home, all I could think about was how sexy you were and I was wondering if you were fucking those other guys."

Vanessa chuckled. "Did Mistress Ivana ever fuck you?" She knew the answer now.

"No," he shook his head and lowered his voice to make sure that he wasn't overheard, "just with the strap-on."

"Well there you go, right? Me either. I never fuck any of the slaves." It was time and she plunged right in. "Although Mistress Ivana and I have been known to play with each other."

He was quiet for a moment but a smile spread across his face. It was obvious that he loved the idea. She could see him imagining the various scenarios where she and Ivana would make love, two women melting into each other's arms, and she realized that she had discovered one of David's secret fantasies.

"Jesus, Vanessa…" It was going to be extremely difficult for him not to make a dash for the men's locker room and masturbate as he contemplated the two of them together. "I didn't know you were bi."

"I'm not, I don't think…" She hadn't ever thought of herself as attracted to all women, just this one in particular. And Mistress Ivana's hold on her was growing. "She's the only woman I've ever been with, actually, but it's incredibly hot."

"That's not fair," he said. He looked as if he was in pain and his erection was obvious in the front of his workout shorts. "I'm so horny for you and now I've got to think about that all day."

"Maybe not…" Vanessa decided that it was time to secure her position as his dominant one once more. "Meet me in the showers in a few minutes."

She left him there and made her way to her locker, stripping quickly and shoving the t-shirt and yoga pants back into the metal bin. She was alone when she entered the tiled area and she waited for him in the corner where they had first made love.

David walked in. His eyes were on her and his cock throbbing as he came to join her.

"Vanessa, I want you so much. I'm so close to cumming just thinking about you and Mistress Ivana."

Vanessa wondered what it would be like if she were there, in person, watching the two of them. She decided that she would let him continue to daydream as she put him in his place.

"On your knees, slave," she said. She used her most authoritative tone and watched as her gorgeous, well-muscled boyfriend quickly obeyed and bent himself into a postulant's position.

"Open your mouth," she commanded. His face was at the perfect height to stare at her full lips and salivate over the glistening droplets that she knew had already appeared. "Are you thinking about me and your Mistress? Are you imagining watching us undress each other?"

He quickly nodded yes and his lips were parted and she knew that she was in command.

"You want to watch while I lick her pussy? That sweet pussy that you could never have?" She whispered and heard him moan with his mounting need.

"I want to watch you touch yourself while you think about my face buried between her lips and my tongue covered in her juices," she said. Just talking about it was turning Vanessa on and she ran her finger around her clit and let the vibration run through her hips. She tensed and waited. David was following her instructions and had begun to masturbate for her. His strong hand was wrapped around his dick and he moved it from the base to the tip, his mouth open and waiting to pleasure her.

The first spurt of her cum surprised him. She could see his eyes open wide as the hot liquid ran down his upper lip and entered his mouth. In a moment, he swallowed and then continued to drink up mouthful after mouthful as she continued to cum on his face. The excess spilled down his chin and ran in a line down the center of his chest. Vanessa watched as the rest of her juices washed his sweaty body and she trembled in excitement.

"Yes, slave. Very good. Drink it all and taste me down inside you," Vanessa murmured and listened to her boyfriend gasp as he took another drink.

He was so close to the edge. It wouldn't take much more to watch as he shook from head to toe with his pent-up release.

"You should be on your knees as you watch me make your Mistress cum all over my face," she moaned.

David cried out and Vanessa watched as long, hot ropes of his salty load burst from the head of his cock and he splattered himself with his climax. Again and again, his cock pulsated with each new wave of his want and Vanessa knew what she needed next.

She was empty and he was shivering on the cold tile.

"Clean me, slave," Vanessa told him and watched as he crawled forward to give her his tongue. She smiled as she had an idea of what needed to happen later that night. It was the one thing she could think of that might just solve both of her problems at once.

*****

Mistress Ivana was waiting for them and Vanessa felt the familiar tingle down her spine as she stared at the beautiful blonde as they walked up the sidewalk. Tonight was going to be a fresh start for her and David and, she hoped, the culmination of all three of their fantasies.

"Vanessa, David," Mistress Ivana greeted her warmly and smirked at her slave. Earlier she had been furious with him for interrupting her when she was with a client. She had warned him sternly on the phone that future outbursts would be met with a severe punishment - maybe she wouldn't even allow him back. As soon as he heard the threat, Vanessa watched as his expression changed to one of remorse. Vanessa had assured the woman that not only was he terribly sorry, but it would never happen again.

"Follow me, please."

Mistress Ivana was taking them both to the dungeon and although Vanessa knew what was in store, David could only guess and she knew he was more than a little scared when he clutched Vanessa's hand with his own trembling one.

"Let's have a little chat then, shall we?" Mistress Ivana stared at David and asked him with a wicked smile, "Where are you manners, slave?"

He quickly got on his knees and looked up at both of the women.

"That's better. I assume that there's no need for us to speak any further about your behavior the other day…" a shadow passed across her face and David shook his head no.

"Good," her heels clicked as she walked around him, "so here's how it's going to be, slave. Vanessa is going to continue to work here with me because the slaves love her. I'm sure you can relate to that," she smirked at him and saw the adoring look he flashed to Vanessa.

"She is very good as a Mistress and now that you know all about her business here, she's quitting her day job and she'll be here full-time."

Mistress Ivana had been telling her from the very beginning that she should but it was only after the incident with David at the health club that she understood that she really was a natural.

"She will see you on her own time because she loves you, I guess…" It was the one point that Ivana had mixed emotions on and the two women had agreed to disagree.

"You also know that Vanessa and I are lovers now," she said. And with that, Ivana reached out and touched Vanessa's face. "Something that she told me is one of your nasty little fantasies, isn't that right, slave?" She waited for David to shake his head yes before she continued. "So, Vanessa has asked that you be allowed to join us once in a while. You'll have to be on your very best behavior, for this to happen. Is that understood?"

David bowed his head and mumbled, "Yes, ma'am."

"Then get undressed, slave, and we'll see just what you can do."

Ivana walked behind Vanessa and wrapped her hands around her waist and let David watch as she touched her belly and then moved her hands down to caress her hips. David couldn't look away and took his clothes off as quickly as he could. His cock was at full attention once he was naked and back in the proper position.

"Now I'm going to put nipple clamps on you, slave." Mistress Ivana held them in her hand and showed him the clips, the delicate chain that connected them dangling. "Something to give you a little added incentive to perform for us."

David thrust his chest up at her and Vanessa purred as she watched the blonde attach the clamps, the teeth digging into his pink, sensitive flesh and pulling at his nipples. David moaned and the precum spilled from his slit and ran down his shaft.

"Now whenever I want you to do something," she yanked the chain that hung against his chiseled abs and the women heard him yelp as the clips dug harder into his skin, "I'll remind you with this."

"Yes, ma'am," he panted and Vanessa saw that he was covered in goosebumps. He was riding the line between pain and pleasure and loving both.

"And just in case you need to be reminded who is in charge, I've got something special for you."

Mistress Ivana was thoroughly enjoying watching him jump and feeling his body tremble under her touch. Vanessa saw what she had taken from the table. It was a cock ring that attached tightly around the base of a man's erection, with tassels and weighted balls that dangled from the device. A Mistress could grasp the tassels with one hand and pull on the man's dick, moving it easily and keeping him achingly hard for as long as wanted. The blonde temptress secured it around David's penis and Vanessa bit her lip as she watched. Seeing the woman's hands on her lover's dick was a breathtaking sight. Knowing that she would have both of them tonight was almost too much.

"Stand up and bend over slave," Mistress Ivana said. She was adjusting the strap-on around her hips, tightening the buckles and Vanessa noticed that she had a very large penis attached to it tonight. "I'm going to fill you up with this cock, so deep that you never forget who your Mistress is." Ivana was covering the shaft with lube and Vanessa watched as it appeared that she was masturbating herself like a man would.

"What do you have to say, slave?" Ivana paused before entering him, simply rubbing the wide, rubber head back and forth along the skin between his cheeks.

"Please fuck me, Mistress. I belong to you," he moaned, pushing his bottom out to show Mistress Ivana his sincerity.

"Now you know what you need to do in order to please me,

don't you slave? I'm going to watch as you lick Vanessa. That will make me very happy. To see her cum all over your face is what I want."

Ivana watched as Vanessa pulled up her skirt, leaning back on the spanking bench, she spread her legs open wide. David was so anxious to do his duty that he lapped at the front of her damp panties with a groan, more than willing to do anything to get the cock he craved.

"Oh, David," Vanessa moaned and pushed her panties down to her knees and threw her head back. Her long, black hair was touching the back of her skirt as she felt his tongue begin to explore her. The thought of Ivana witnessing her grinding her hips against his face and riding his wet mouth was almost too much. She knew she was close to an orgasm already and he had just begun.

David cried out with an open mouth. The sound was loud as he was penetrated by the leather-clad woman behind him and Vanessa watched him move his bottom to Ivana's tempo as she thrust inside. The head had already pushed through his tight hole and half of the enormous shaft and Vanessa knew that David would take every inch of her lover's girth as he subjugated himself for both women.

"Your boyfriend's little asshole is so tight," Ivana said staring at Vanessa and it seemed as if the woman was imagining fucking her with the strap-on instead. Her rubber cock was taking David completely, rocking him back and forth so that he went up on the balls of his feet the deeper she was inside. Vanessa purred. His tongue was the perfect foreplay. Her clit was swollen with cum and she would coat his lips and tongue with her sweet release before offering herself to the woman who would make her melt under her caress.

Vanessa looked down at David and ran her fingers through his hair as she moved her hips. She knew that the night was just beginning and the possibilities were endless. She should really thank him later, she thought, when the two of them were alone once more.

For now, she wrapped her fingers in his hair and pushed his face into her crotch. It was exactly what he wanted and what his Mistress would do.

His *new* Mistress.

The End

*****

If you've enjoyed this book, please **leave a review**, and let me know your thoughts!

Printed in Great Britain
by Amazon